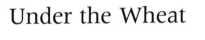

Under the Wheat

Winner of the Drue Heinz Literature Prize 1986

UNDER THE WHEAT

RICK DeMARINIS

University of Pittsburgh Press

Published by the University of Pittsburgh Press, Pittsburgh, Pa., 15260
Copyright © 1986, Rick DeMarinis
Feffer and Simons, Inc., London
Manufactured in the United States of America

Library of Congress Cataloging-in-Publication Data

DeMarinis, Rick, 1934–
    Under the Wheat.

    "Winner of the Drue Heinz literature prize, 1986"—T.p. verso.
    I. Title.
PS3554.E4554U5 1986   813'.54   86-7007
ISBN 0-8229-3544-9

"Under the Wheat" originally appeared in *The Iowa Review*, "The Smile of a Turtle"
was first published in *Grand Street*, "Weeds" is reprinted from *Rocky Mountain
Magazine*, "Life Between Meals" was originally published in *Cavalier*, "Blind
Euchre" originally appeared in *Esquire* under the title, "A Game Without Children," and "Billy Ducks Among the Pharaohs" first appeared in *CutBank*.

Hard to salute each other
harder to describe each other
and hardest to look at each other
at our destination.

—Amos Tutuola, *The Palm-Wine Drinkard*

Contents

Under the Wheat

DOWN IN D-3 I watch the sky gunning through the aperture ninety-odd feet above my head. The missiles are ten months away, and I am lying on my back listening to the sump. From the bottom of a hole, where the weather is always the same cool sixty-four degrees, plus or minus two, I like to relax and watch the clouds slide through the circle of blue light. I have plenty of time to kill. The aperture is about fifteen feet wide. About the size of a silver dollar from here. A hawk just drifted by. Eagle. Crow. Small cumulus. Nothing. Nothing. Wrapper.

Hot again today, and the sky is drifting across the hole, left to right, a slow thick wind that doesn't gust. When it gusts, it's usually from Canada. Fierce, with hail the size of eyeballs. I've seen wheat go down. Acres and acres of useless straw.

But sometimes it comes out of the southeast, from Bismarck, bringing ten-mile-high anvils with it, and you find yourself looking for funnels. This is not tornado country to speak of. The tornado path is to the south and west of here. They walk up from Bismarck and farther south and peter out on the Montana border, rarely touching ground anywhere near this latitude. Still, you keep an eye peeled. I've seen them put down gray fingers to the west, not quite touching but close enough to make you want to find a hole. They say it sounds like freight trains in your yard. I wouldn't know. We are from the coast, where the weather is stable and always predictable because of the ocean. We are trying to adjust.

4

I make five hundred a week doing this, driving a company pickup from hole to hole, checking out the sump pumps. I've found only one failure in two months. Twenty feet of black water in the hole and rising. It's the company's biggest headache. The high water table of North Dakota. You can dig twelve feet in any field and have yourself a well. You can dig yourself a shallow hole, come back in a few days and drink. That's why the farmers here have it made. Except for hail. Mostly they are Russians, these farmers.

Karen wants to go back. I have to remind her it's only for one year. Ten more months. Five hundred a week for a year. But she misses things. The city, her music lessons, movies, the beach, excitement. We live fairly close to a town, but it's one you will never hear of, unless a local goes wild and chainsaws all six members of his family. The movie theater has shown *Bush*

Pilot, Red Skies of Montana, Ice Palace, and *Kon Tiki* so far. These are movies we would not ordinarily pay money to see. She has taken to long walks in the evenings to work out her moods, which are getting harder and harder for me to pretend aren't there. I get time and a half on Saturdays, double time Sundays and holidays, and thirteen dollars per diem for the inconvenience of relocating all the way from Oxnard, California. That comes to a lot. You don't walk away from a gold mine like that. I try to tell Karen she has to make the effort, adjust. North Dakota isn't all that bad. As a matter of fact, I sort of enjoy the area. Maybe I am more adaptable. We live close to a large brown lake, an earthfill dam loaded with northern pike. I bought myself a little boat and often go out to troll a bit before the car pool comes by. The freezer is crammed with fish, not one under five pounds.

5

There's a ghost town on the other side of the lake. The houses were built for the men who worked on the dam. That was years ago. They are paintless now, weeds up to the rotten sills. No glass in the windows, but here and there a rag of drape. Sometimes I take my boat across the lake to the ghost town. I walk the overgrown streets and look into the windows. Sometimes something moves. Rats. Gophers. Wind. Loose boards. Sometimes nothing.

When the weather is out of Canada you can watch it move south, coming like a giant roll of silver dough on the horizon. It gets bigger fast and then you'd better find cover. If the cloud is curdled underneath, you know it means hail. The wind can gust to one hundred knots. It scares Karen. I tell her there's nothing to worry about. Our trailer is on a good foundation and tied down tight. But she has this dream of being uprooted and of flying away in such a wind. She sees her broken body caught in a tree, magpies picking at it. I tell her the trailer will definitely not budge. Still, she gets wild-eyed and can't light a cigarette.

6

We're sitting at the dinette table looking out the window, watching the front arrive. You can feel the trailer bucking like a boat at its moorings. Lightning is stroking the blond fields a mile away. To the southeast, I can see a gray finger reaching down. This is unusual, I admit. But I say nothing to Karen. It looks like the two fronts are going to butt heads straight over the trailer park. It's getting dark fast. Something splits the sky behind the trailer and big hail pours out. The streets of the park are white and jumping under the black sky. Karen has her hands up to her ears. There's a stampede on our tin roof. Two TV antennas fold at the same time in a dead faint. A jagged Y of lightning strikes so close you can smell it. Electric steam. Karen is wild, screaming. I can't hear her. Our garbage cans are rising. They are floating past the windows into a flattened wheat field. This is something. Karen's face is closed. She doesn't enjoy it at all, not at all.

I'm tooling around in third on the usual bad road, enjoying the lurches, rolls, and twists. I would not do this to my own truck. The fields I'm driving through are wasted. Head-on with the sky and the sky never loses. I've passed a few unhappy looking farmers standing in their fields with their hands in their pockets, faces frozen in an expression of disgust, spitting. Toward D-8, just over a rise and down into a narrow gulch, I found a true glacier. It was made out of hail stones welded together by their own impact. It hadn't begun to melt yet. Four feet thick and maybe thirty feet long. You can stand on it and shade your eyes from the white glare. You could tell yourself you are inside the arctic circle. What is this, the return of the ice age?

7

Karen did not cook tonight. Another "mood." I poke around in the fridge. I don't know what to say to her anymore. I know it's hard. I can understand that. This is not Oxnard. I'll give her that. I'm the first to admit it. I pop a beer and sit down at the table opposite her. Our eyes don't meet. They haven't for weeks. We are like two magnetic north poles, repelling each other for invisible reasons. Last night in bed I touched her. She went stiff. She didn't have to say a word. I took my hand back. I got the message. There was the hum of the air conditioner and nothing else. The world could have been filled with dead bodies. I turned on the lights. She got up and lit a cigarette after two tries. Nerves. "I'm going for a walk, Lloyd," she said, checking the sky. "Maybe we should have a baby?" I said. "I'm making plenty of money." But she looked at me as if I had picked up an ax.

I would like to know where she finds to go and what she finds to do there. She hates the town worse than the trailer park. The trailer park has a rec hall and a social club for the wives. But she won't take advantage of that. I know the neighbors are talking. They think she's a snob. They think I spoil her. After she left I went out on the porch and drank eleven beers. Let them talk.

8

Three farm kids. Just standing outside the locked gate of D-4. "What do you kids want?" I know what they want. A "look-see." Security measures are in effect, but what the hell. There is nothing here yet but a ninety-foot hole with a tarp on it and a sump pump in the bottom. They are excited when I open the access hatch and invite them to climb down the narrow steel ladder to the bottom. They want to know what ICBM stands for. What is a warhead? How fast is it? How do you know if it's really going to smear the right town? What if it went straight up and came straight down? Can you hit the moon? "Look at the sky up there, kids," I tell them. "Lie on your backs, like this, and after a while you sort of get the feeling you're looking *down*, from on top of it." The kids lie down on the concrete. Kids have a way of giving all their attention to something interesting. I swear them to secrecy, not for my protection, because who cares, but because it will make their day. They will run home, busting with secret info. I drive off to D-9, where the sump trouble was.

Caught three lunkers this morning. All over twenty-four inches. It's 7:00 A.M. now and I'm on Ruby Street, the ghost town. The streets are all named after stones. Why I don't know. This is nothing like anything we have on the coast. Karen doesn't like the climate or the people and the flat sky presses down on her from all sides and gives her bad dreams, sleeping and awake. But what can I *do?*

I'm on Onyx Street, number 49, a two-bedroom bungalow with a few pieces of furniture left in it. There is a chest of drawers in the bedroom, a bed with a rotten gray mattress. There is a closet with a raggedy slip in it. The slip has brown water stains on it that look like burns. In the bottom of the chest is a magazine, yellow with age. *Secret Confessions.* I can imagine the woman who lived here with her husband. Not much like Karen at all. But what did she do while her husband was off working on the dam? Did she stand at this window in her slip and wish she were back in Oxnard? Did she cry her eyes out on this bed and think crazy thoughts? Where is she now? Does she think, "This is July 15, 1962, and I am glad I am not in North Dakota anymore"? Did she take long walks at night and not cook? I have an impulse to do something odd, and do it.

When a thunderhead passes over a cyclone fence

9

that surrounds a site, such as the one passing over D-6 now, you can hear the wire hiss with nervous electrons. It scares me because the fence is a perfect lightning rod, a good conductor. But I stay on my toes. Sometimes, when a big cumulus is overhead stroking the area and roaring, I'll just stay put in my truck until it's had its fun.

10 Because this is Sunday, I am making better than twelve dollars an hour. I'm driving through a small farming community called Spacebow. A Russian word, I think, because you're supposed to pronounce the *e*. No one I know does. Shade trees on every street. A Russian church here, grain elevator there. No wind. Hot for 9:00 A.M. Men dressed in Sunday black. Ladies in their best. Kids looking uncomfortable and controlled. Even the dogs are behaving. There is a woman, manless I think, because I've seen her before, always alone on her porch, eyes on something far away. A "thinker." Before today I've only waved hello. First one finger off the wheel, nod, then around the block once again and the whole hand out the window and a smile. That was last week. After the first turn past her place today she waves back. A weak hand at first, as if she's not sure that's what I meant. But after a few times around the block she knows that's what I meant. And so I'm stopping. I'm going to ask for a cup of cold water. I'm thirsty anyway. Maybe all this sounds hokey to you if you are from some big town like Oxnard, but this is not a big town like Oxnard.

Her name is Myrna Dan. That last name must be a
pruned-down version of Danielovitch or something
because the people here are mostly Russians. She is
thirty-two, a widow, one brat. A two-year-old named
"Piper," crusty with food. She owns a small farm here
but there is no one to work it. She has a decent allot-
ment from the U.S. government and a vegetable garden. If you are from the coast you would not stop what
you were doing to look at her. Her hands are square
and the fingers stubby, made for rough wooden
handles. Hips like gateposts.   11

No supper again. Karen left a note. "Lloyd, I am
going for a walk. There are some cold cuts in the
fridge." It wasn't even signed. Just like that. One of
these days on one of her walks she is going to get
caught by the sky which can change on you in a
minute.

Bill Finkel made a remark on the way in to the dis-
patch center. It was a little personal and coming from
anybody else I would have called him on it. But he is
the lead engineer, the boss. A few of the other guys
grinned behind their hands. How do I know where she
goes or why? I am not a swami. If it settles her nerves,
why should I push it? I've thought of sending her to
Ventura to live with her mother for a while, but her
mother is getting senile and has taken to writing mean
letters. I tell Karen the old lady is around the bend,
don't take those letters too seriously. But what's the use

when the letters come in like clockwork, once a week, page after page of nasty accusations in a big, inch-high scrawl, like a kid's, naming things that never happened. Karen takes it hard, no matter what I say, as if what the old lady says is true.

Spacebow looks deserted. It isn't. The men are off in the fields, the women are inside working toward evening. Too hot outside even for the dogs who are sleeping under the porches. Ninety-nine. I stopped for water at Myrna's. Do you want to see a missile silo? Sure, she said, goddamn right, just like that. I have an extra hard hat in the truck but she doesn't have to wear it if she doesn't want to. Regulations at this stage of the program are a little pointless. Just a hole with a sump in it. Of course you can fall into it and get yourself killed. That's about the only danger. But there are no regulations that can save you from your own stupidity. Last winter when these holes were being dug, a kid walked out on a tarp. The tarp was covered with light snow and he couldn't tell where the ground ended and the hole began. He dropped the whole ninety feet and his hard hat did not save his ass. Myrna is impressed with this story. She is very anxious to see one. D-7 is closest to Spacebow, only a mile out of town. It isn't on my schedule today, but so what. I hand her the orange hat. She has trouble with the chin strap. I help her cinch it. Piper wants to wear it too and grabs at the straps, whining. Myrna has big jaws. Strong. But not in an ugly way.

12

I tell her the story about Jack Stern, the Jewish quality control man from St. Louis who took flying lessons because he wanted to be able to get to a decent-sized city in a hurry whenever he felt the need. This flat empty farm land made his ulcer flare. He didn't know how to drive a car, and yet there he was, tearing around the sky in a Bonanza. One day he flew into a giant hammerhead—thinking, I guess, that a cloud like that is nothing but a lot of water vapor, no matter what shape it has or how big—and was never heard from again. That cloud ate him and the Bonanza. At the airport up in Minot they picked up two words on the emergency frequency, "Oh no," then static.

13

I tell her the story about the motor pool secretary who shot her husband once in the neck and twice in the foot with a target pistol while he slept. Both of them pulling down good money, too. I tell her the one about the one that got away. A northern as big as a shark. Pulled me and my boat a mile before my twelve-pound test monofilament snapped. She gives me a sidelong glance and makes a buzzing sound as if to say, *That* one takes the cake, Mister! We are on the bottom of D-7, watching the circle of sky, lying on our backs.

The trailer *stinks*. I could smell it from the street as soon as I got out of Bill Finkel's car. Fish heads. *Heads!* I guess they've been sitting there like that most of the afternoon. Just the big alligator jaws of my big beautiful pikes, but not the bodies. A platter of them, uncooked, drying out, and getting high. Knife, fork, napkin, glass. I'd like to know what goes on inside her head, what passes for thinking in there. The note: "Lloyd, eat your fill." Not signed. Is this supposed to be humor? I fail to get the point of it. I have to carry the mess to the garbage cans without breathing. A wind has come up. From the southeast. A big white fire is blazing in the sky over my shoulder. You can hear the far-off rumble, like a whale grunting. I squint west, checking for funnels.

14

Trouble in D-7. Busted sump. I pick up Myrna and Piper and head for the hole. It's a nice day for a drive. It could be a bearing seizure, but that's only a percentage guess. I unlock the gate and we drive to the edge of it. Space-age artillery, I explain, as we stand on the lip of D-7, feeling the vertigo. The tarp is off for maintenance and the hole is solid black. If you let your imagination run, you might see it as bottomless. The "Pit" itself. Myrna is holding Piper back. Piper is whining, she wants to see the hole. Myrna has to slap her away, scolding. I drain my beer and let the can drop. I don't hear it hit. Not even a splash. I grab the fussing kid and hold her out over the hole. "Have yourself a *good* look, brat," I say. I hold her by the ankle with one hand. She is paralyzed. Myrna goes so white I have to smile. "Oh wait," she says. "Please, Lloyd. No." As if I ever would.

Myrna wants to see the D-flight control center. I ask her if she has claustrophobia. She laughs, but it's no joke. That far below the surface inside that capsule behind an eight-ton door can be upsetting if you're susceptible to confinement. The elevator is slow and heavy, designed to haul equipment. The door opens on a dimly lit room. Spooky. There's crated gear scattered around. And there is the door, one yard thick to withstand the shock waves from the Bomb. I wheel it open. Piper whines, her big eyes distrustful. There is a musty smell in the dank air. The lights and blower are on now, but it will take a while for the air to freshen itself up. I wheel the big door shut. It can't latch yet, but Myrna is impressed. I explain to her what goes on in here. We sit down at the console. I show her where the launch enabling switches will be and why it will take two people together to launch an attack, the chairs fifteen feet apart and both switches turned for a several-second count before the firing sequence can start, in case one guy goes berserk and decides to end the world because his old lady has been holding out on him, or just for the hell of it, given human nature. I show her the escape hole. It's loaded with ordinary sand. You pull this chain and the sand dumps into the capsule. Then you climb up the tube that held the sand into someone's wheat field. I show her the toilet and the little kitchen. I can see there is something on her mind. Isolated places make you think of weird things. It's happened to me more than once. Not here, but in the ghost town on the other side of the lake.

Topside the weather has changed. The sky is the color of pikebelly, wind rising from the southeast. To the west I can see stubby funnels pushing down from

15

the overcast, but only so far. It looks like the clouds are growing roots. We have to run back to the truck in the rain, Piper screaming on Myrna's hip. A heavy bolt strikes less than a mile away. A blue fireball sizzles where it hits. Smell the ozone. It makes me sneeze.

This is the second day she's been gone. I don't know where or how. All her clothes are here. She doesn't have any money. I don't know what to do. There is no police station. Do I call her mother? Do I notify the FBI? The highway patrol? Bill Finkel?

16

Everybody in the car pool knows but won't say a word, out of respect for my feelings. Bill Finkel has other things on his mind. He is worried about rumored economy measures in the assembly and check-out program next year. It has nothing to do with me. My job ends before that phase begins. I guess she went back to Oxnard, or maybe Ventura. But how?

We are in the D-flight control center. Myrna, with her hard hat cocked to one side, wants to fool around with the incomplete equipment. Piper is with her grandma. We are seated at the control console and she is pretending to work her switch. She has me pretend to work my switch. She wants to launch the entire flight of missiles, D-1 through D-10 at Cuba or Panama. Why Cuba and Panama? I ask. What about Russia? Why not Cuba or Panama? she says. Besides, I have Russian blood. Everyone around here has Russian blood. No, it's Cuba and Panama. Just think of the looks on their faces. All those people lying in the sun on the decks of those big white holiday boats, the coolies out in the cane fields, the tinhorn generals, the whole shiteree. They'll look up trying to shade their eyes but they won't be able to. What in hell is this all about they'll say, then *zap*, poof, *gone*.

I feel it too, craziness like hers. What if I couldn't get that eight-ton door open, Myrna? I see her hard hat wobble, her lip drop. What if? Just what *if?* She puts her arms around me and our hard hats click. She is one strong woman.

Lloyd, Lloyd, she says.

Yo.

Jesus.

Easy.

Lloyd!

Bingo.

It's good down here—no *rules*—and she goes berserk. But later she is calm and up to mischief again. I recognize the look now. Okay, I tell her. What *next,* Myrna? She wants to do something halfway nasty. This, believe me, doesn't surprise me at all.

I'm sitting on the steel floor listening to the blower and waiting for Myrna to finish her business. I'm trying hard to picture what the weather is doing topside. It's not easy to do. It could be clear and calm and blue or it could be wild. There could be a high, thin overcast or there could be nothing. You just can't know when you're this far under the wheat. I can hear her trying to work the little chrome lever, even though I told her

17

there's no plumbing yet. Some maintenance yokel is going to find Myrna's "surprise." She comes out, pretending to be sheepish, but I can see that the little joke tickles her.

Something takes my hook and strips off ten yards of line then stops dead. Snag. I reel in. The pole is bent double and the line is singing. Then something lets go but it isn't the line because I'm still snagged. It breaks the surface, a lady's shoe. It's brown and white with a short heel. I toss it into the bottom of the boat. The water is shallow here, and clear. There's something dark and wide under me like a shadow on the water. An old farmhouse, submerged when the dam filled. There's a deep current around the structure. I can see fence, tires, an old truck, feed pens. There is a fat farmer in the yard staring up at me, checking the weather, and I jump away from him, almost tipping the boat. My heart feels tangled in my ribs. But it's only a stump with arms.

The current takes my boat in easy circles. A swimmer would be in serious trouble. I crank up the engine and head back. No fish today. So be it. Sometimes you come home empty-handed. The shoe is new, stylish, and was made in Spain.

I'm standing on the buckled porch of 49 Onyx Street. Myrna is inside reading *Secret Confessions:* "What My Don Must Never Know." The sky is bad. The lake is bad. It will be a while before we can cross back. I knock

18

on the door, as we planned. Myrna is on the bed in the stained, raggedy slip, giggling. "Listen to this dogshit, Lloyd," she says. But I'm not in the mood for weird stories. "I brought you something, honey," I say. She looks at the soggy shoe. "That?" But she agrees to try it on, anyway. I feel like my own ghost, bumping into the familiar but run-down walls of my old house in the middle of nowhere, and I remember my hatred of it. "Hurry up," I say, my voice true as a razor.

A thick tube hairy with rain is snaking out of the sky 19 less than a mile away. Is it going to touch? "They never do, Lloyd. This isn't Kansas. Will you please listen to this dogshit?" Something about a pregnant high school girl, Dee, locked in a toilet with a knitting needle. Something about this Don who believes in purity. Something about bright red blood. Something about ministers and mothers and old-fashioned shame. I'm not listening, even when Dee slides the big needle in. I have to keep watch on the sky, because there is a first time for everything, even if this is not Kansas. The wind is stripping shingles from every roof I see. A long board is spinning like a slow propeller. The funnel is behind a bluff, holding back. But I can hear it, the freight trains. Myrna is standing behind me, running a knuckle up and down my back. "Hi, darling," she says. "Want to know what I did while you were out working on the dam today?" The dark tube has begun to move out from behind the bluff, but I'm not sure which way. "Tell me," I say. "Tell me."

Good Wars

MY FATHER CAME HOME from the Second World War empty. He didn't look empty. He was much larger than when he went away, three years earlier. When he left us for the war, he was a lean twenty-seven-year-old, full of stories and jokes that made me and my little brother Woodrow laugh until we hurt. When he came home he was thick with fat and he looked forty. His arms stuck out from his sides, his legs were tight in his wool army pants, and his belly rolled out in front of him like a grievous load someone had forced him to bear. Even so, there was nothing inside him any more, nothing for us. It was as if an over-weight impostor was trying to pass himself off as our happy Dad. We won that war, but he came home glum as the losers.

I didn't understand how war could make someone fat or how victory could make him empty. Woodrow and I thought his antics would be twice as good, now that he'd been to war and had come home safely, but we were wrong. We waited for his long, preposterous stories, his winks and chuckles, but he only sat unmoving in his easy chair, reading or dozing. Or he would go for long walks through town, refusing to let either me or Woodrow tag along. We nagged and pulled at his sleeve. We tried to remind him how generous he had once been with his time, but he acted as if we weren't really there. He didn't know us anymore. He had forgotten us.

It was hard to accept. I reminded him of his story about the airliner that ran out of gas and went down in the Gobi desert and how all the men passengers donated their suspenders so that the pilot could make windup motors out of them that would turn the propellers and allow the plane to fly everyone back to civilization, but he just looked mildly alarmed, as though only some kind of irresponsible idiot would tell such lies to children. We whined to Mother but she hushed us, saying, "Daddy isn't himself yet. He'll be all right, but we need to give him time. He saw terrible things overseas."

We gave him time. But as the years passed he became more sullen and withdrawn. He acted as if nothing around him had a real existence, including his wife and children. We were just smokey shapes drifting around him and sometimes pestering the quiet empty spaces that occupied his reverie. The things he had seen in Europe had hollowed out the once substantial elements of his prewar world. Then one day he packed a single suitcase and left home without a word of explanation, apology, or good-bye.

After a few months Mother gave up on him. Then she, too, became sullen and indifferent. I didn't know if she was just bitter for being abandoned or if the emptiness of my father had been a contagious thing that had infected her, too. She put on weight and the heavier she got the more distracted and heedless of the world around her she became. I looked for signs of it in Woodrow and myself. Could the same thing infect us? I struck poses in the bathroom mirror that reminded me of my father. I pushed my belly out, wondering if it could bloat. I imagined myself empty, and, imagining it, I *felt* it. Something solid but invisible rose up from my legs, gathered momentum, and assaulted my stomach and chest. It flew into my throat. My mouth fell open and I heard it screech over my tongue and past my teeth.

"What's the matter with you, Bernard?" Mother asked through the bathroom door, tapping it lightly. It was a dutiful question, something a mother would ask. But it was empty of care. "Are you getting sick, Bernard?"

"No, I'm not getting sick," I said. I told her that I was only laughing. "I just remembered a joke," I said, my face in the toilet, the gleaming wet porcelain hollowing out my words until they became brittle shells of sound.

Time drained some of Mother's bitterness away. She began to have dates now and then. The men she dated seemed generally lifeless to me. I would watch Mother and her dates sitting at the kitchen table over beer and

25

potato chips talking in bored voices about weather or work or relatives. One man named Rolly Spydell I remember because of his greenish complexion and his busy, nicotine-stained fingers. He would drum the table impatiently when listening to Mother, and when he talked, his fingers would punch little emphatic holes in the air. Rolly drove a long black Packard that drifted down our street like an ebony coffin that had been accidentally launched into a slow river. Mother and Rolly would sit in the big car together in the driveway after a date, talking with their mouths almost shut and staring out the windshield as if at the dead immensity of infinite space.

26

Another man she dated was critical of nearly everything. His caustic remarks would descend, in stages, from the loftier subjects of the national government and the state of public morality, to the little things he found personally offensive in his everyday life. Criticism was the only form of expression that gave him the appearance of having purpose and energy. When the subject of conversation was not open to criticism he became inarticulate and confused or openly bored. Words, to him, were small, cruelly sharp instruments to be used only for cutting away the fat from the lean, and sometimes the lean from bone. He once said out loud that criticism was his gift. He looked as though he was waiting for someone to pin a medal on him after he said this.

A man I remember only as "Pincher" seemed, at first, to be full of life and good fun. He was a big pink man with a round hairless head. He was always winking at us and sticking his tongue into his cheek as if everything was a joke. He brought us gifts. He brought Woodrow an imitation Samurai sword he'd bought in Tokyo during the Occupation. He gave me a Red Ryder BB rifle. We called him "Pincher" because he liked to give us pinches. He pinched Woodrow and he pinched me. He pinched Mother until she begged him to stop. He pinched expertly and he pinched hard. Once I looked at the back of my arm and saw the blue imprint of his thumb and forefinger. He made Woodrow cry. "Don't be a baby, Woody," he laughed, as Woodrow ran from the house screaming. Though I was several years older than Woodrow, Pincher made me cry once, too. I turned away from him so that he wouldn't see the quick well of tears in my eyes, but he forced me to face him. He needed to see those tears. They were important to him. Then he winked, stuck his tongue into his cheek, and tousled my hair. One day I accidentally caught Mother coming out of the bathroom in her underwear and saw that her arms and shoulders, as well as her thighs, were leopard-spotted with blue and yellowing welts.

27

About this time a shy bully at school named Dolph Hubler singled me out to be his latest victim. At fifteen I wasn't as big or as courageous as I wanted to be. I was a disappointment to myself at five feet seven inches tall and one hundred and thirty pounds. Dolph, who had been set back a grade or two, was man-sized. He was close to six feet and probably weighed two hundred pounds. He was big and clumsy and forced by his parents to wear faded bib overalls and oversized oxblood wing tip shoes that were obvious hand-me-downs from his father or older brothers. Dolph wasn't a natural bully, but had been forced into the role because of the sly smirks his appearance aroused. To keep these smirks at a respectful distance, Dolph would single someone out now and then in random reprisal.

Dolph would look for me in the crowd of kids loitering in the school yard before the first bell. When he found me, he'd slap the books out of my hands and then show me, and whoever else might be interested, his big raw fist. He made the top middle knuckle protrude as if introducing me to it. Then he would punch my shoulder hard enough to jar my collar bones. The first time he did this I was so stunned and panic-stricken that I couldn't talk or move. Filled with a sick dread I hadn't known before, I smiled at him. My smile was irrational since it had no bearing on my true inner state. Dolph towered over me, annoyed by this inappropriate smile. He had the body of a middle-aged beer drinker. His ears were big and fleshy and when he walked, he waddled from side to side, the palms of his hands facing backwards, apelike.

Everyone was afraid of him. Each morning when he approached, my friends would drift away as if they had pressing business on the other side of the school yard. None of them wanted to show partisanship for me, knowing that such a foolhardy gesture could only attract attention to themselves as a possible source of future victims. I ran with a clique of intrinsically cautious boys who liked to pose in rugged approximations of James Dean, Marlon Brando, and Aldo Ray, hoping to distract one another from the homely truth about themselves. They would slouch in groups, thumbs hooked insolently into the belt loops of their Levi's, saying, "Well then there now," in the breezy, dreamy way James Dean said it in *Rebel Without a Cause.* They would repeat this phrase to each other tirelessly, as if it were real conversation, packs of Chesterfields, Camels, or Lucky Strikes rolled into the sleeves of their T-shirts. Though they moaned at passing girls with the sexual menace of Marlon Brando, they would marry the first or second girl they slept with. They were in love with safety. After high school, they would pursue college deferments from the draft. They would plan sensible careers. And they would do nothing to attract attention to themselves, knowing instinctively that Dolph Hubler existed in the world as a *principle,* a mindlessly vengeful force, darkly determined to inflict pain and humiliation at random but always gravitating to the most visible targets.

29

    Dolph Hubler put a serious crimp in the safe allegiances I was in the process of adopting. Dolph was my first crisis in personal relationships. There was no way around him. I couldn't put him out of my mind. I dreamed about him. In one of my dreams we went fishing together. We were wading in a stream. Suddenly I realized the fishing trip had been a ruse. Neither of us had poles. He was going to drown me. I saw it in his face as he waded toward me. I woke up, fighting for high ground.

Dolph homed in on me each morning, knuckle up-raised, his small colorless eyes unblinking. My cringe was internal, not visible, but Dolph perceived it anyway and rejoiced in it. Outwardly I pretended that the morning ritual between us was all in good fun and that his shoulder punches were not a great inconvenience. He would hit me and I would say, "Well then there now Dolph," in the casual, unhurried manner of James Dean. It was the way I had chosen to save face. All my friends approved of it. "Attaway, Bernie," said one of them, his voice manfully hoarse in the whispering style of Aldo Ray. "You showed that pissant, Bernie." Such congratulations were offered, of course, only after Dolph had lumbered out of earshot.

The trouble with my strategy, though, was that while it was face-saving to me, it was frustrating to Dolph. He needed to strip me of my James Dean front and expose me to our wide audience as a sissy, maybe even as a crybaby. And so he increased the force of his punches until my lower lip began to tremble under the easy anarchy of my cool smile. He made an ear-piercing, falling-bomb whistle to dramatize the ballistic arc of his punch and then the bomb-blast boom when the red knuckle sank into my shoulder deep enough to knock bone. I felt my well-greased hair lifted by impact into comical arrangements. My shoulder became a blue disaster zone of pulverized meat.

Mother's latest boyfriend was a tiny, wiry man named Ducky Tillinghast. Ducky was smaller than me but he radiated toughness. He'd been in the navy for twenty years and had once been featherweight champ of the Sixth Fleet. Somehow he'd caught wind of my difficulties with Dolph Hubler. One evening, after we'd all had dinner together, he took me aside. "Bullies are almost always yellow, Bernard," he said somberly. "I say almost always because you never know for sure. There's the chance that you have drawn the one in ten who is everything he says he is. But I guarantee you, son, most of them are pushovers when you deal with them properly. Why do you think he picked you, someone half his size?"

Ducky gave me a ten-minute boxing lesson I didn't want. I had no intention of hitting Dolph Hubler back. As I watched Ducky holding up his little fists and shuffling his feet around, I felt a large surge of contempt. Dolph Hubler could pick Ducky up by the nape of his neck and throw him over the school yard fence. It was ludicrous to me, this pint-size man encouraging me to fight a monster the two of us together wouldn't have been able to handle. I guess I was sneering a little at him, but he paid no attention to it.

"You set up the right with the left," he said, pawing at the air. "You stick stick stick with the left, then you come over and stake him with the right." He danced in front of me like a midget Sugar Ray Robinson. He showed me how to make a left jab snap like a flicked whip and how to put body weight into my right. He

31

finally took note of my half-hearted and somewhat dis-respectful attitude. It bothered him. We were out in the backyard. He offered me a cigarette. We smoked and talked in the dark among the throbbing crickets. "Look, Bernard," he said after a while. "I can show you a thousand tricks, but if you don't have the belly for a fight, then none of them can help you."

I hated him suddenly. I was glad it was too dark for him to see how red my face had become or how my lip was quivering.

32   "I'll tell you this, though, Bernard," he said. "If you let it go on, you will eat so much dirt that eventually you will come to think it's the only item on the menu. The world is already full of men like that."

I saw Mother frowning at the cigarette in my hand. She was at the kitchen window, doing the dishes. I took a deep drag, making the burning tip glow brightly so that it would illuminate my face which was once again placid with contempt.

"What do you have to lose, Bernard?" Ducky said.

I pictured the things I had to lose. I saw my teeth sprinkled on the asphalt school yard. I saw my ripped shirt spotted with red. And I saw worse. I saw Dolph dragging me around the school yard by my ankles as girls in their crisp skirts and saddle shoes giggled with forbidden excitement. It was clear to me that I had an awful lot to lose. My friends would understand this. They were going to live by an understanding of it all their lives. They had already become experts in their midteens at cutting their losses. They were learning very quickly how to face the world with a handy smile while the world beat them slowly into pablum.

So, when I actually hit Dolph Hubler, no one was more surprised than me. I'd already decided that endurance was a greater virtue than the will to retaliate. I'd simply outlast Dolph. He'd get bored eventually and find someone more promising. But one morning my fake James Dean indifference suddenly collapsed. Dolph was especially disgruntled with my passive response to his ballistic punches and so he doubled the force and the rate of delivery until he was panting with effort. I felt myself caving in. Something terrible was about to happen—I was going to cry or run away or beg him to stop. To prevent this I dipped my shoulder away from his falling fist. This small act of resistance alarmed him. He wasn't prepared for it. His big, heavily freckled face sagged with surprise. Before I fully understood the movement that dipping my shoulder had started, my left hand was flicking at his nose. It snapped like a whip, just as Ducky said it would. The feel of soft, yielding flesh under my knuckles was a revelation to me. It was equivalent in magnitude to my discovery two years earlier of masturbation. It was a new, illicit pleasure of the body.

Surprise continued to mount in Dolph's face. Then it began to change into horror. His hands hung helplessly at his sides, paralyzed by this impossible turn of events. I took the opportunity to step toward him. My right foot planted, I was able to put my entire body weight into my right hand. It bounced off his nose with a wet

33

meaty thump. Dolph sat down. Blood spigoted from a nostril, tears rolled from his eyes.

My friends congratulated me loudly but their praise was tempered by dismay. An element of disapproval undermined the barking shouts that celebrated my victory. Eventually they drifted away from me. I was no longer one of them, I was untrustworthy, perhaps dangerous. I began to associate with a new, rowdier group. They were grittier than my old friends, but they hadn't been gritty enough to challenge Dolph Hubler.

34   Exposed now for what he was, Dolph became the school clown. My new friend, Art Bannister, humiliated Dolph on a daily basis. He would punch Dolph on the arms or stomach and make him cry. Art declared one morning to an audience of hooting girls from the seedier section of town that Dolph would be their "Slave for a Day." He would carry books, run errands, and open doors. Dolph Hubler in his oversized oxblood wing tip hand-me-downs became a living joke. How he had ever been feared was so great a mystery that we could only deal with it by forgetting it. His past freedom to spread terror was simply erased from the collective school yard memory.

Shortly after Mother broke up with Ducky Tillinghast, she took a job as hostess in a restaurant called Chez Frenchy. Her salary wasn't much but she did very well in tips. Chez Frenchy was owned by Frenchy Bigelow, a tall, dark, hairy man who liked to wear jewelry, especially diamonds. He had a diamond stick pin, a wristwatch with diamond hours, a large signet ring with a diamond center, and a pinky ring with a big sapphire in it.

Frenchy liked to talk. He told me he'd been in the war, working with the French Resistance. He'd been a right-hand man to Pierre-Michel Rayon, the famous underground leader. He had an autographed picture of Rayon. The picture looked as if it had been torn out of a magazine and the autograph was an unreadable cork-screw of blue ink. Frenchy was a friendly man who liked to recount his wartime experiences. The war fas- 35 cinated me and I liked to listen to him tell about it. He said that he'd been responsible for blowing up three German tanks and an entire railroad bridge, complete with supply train. He said he killed an SS colonel with his bare hands. He showed me his large, hairy hands and closed them slowly into fists, demonstrating their life-extinguishing power. He regarded these lethal fists with a melancholy that spoke of war's enduring sor-row. He told me how to make a bomb out of a mixture of sugar, acid, and calcium chlorate that could be used to incinerate a German staff car. He explained how to determine the structural weaknesses of railroad trestles. He recalled fondly the selfless courage of the Parisian graffiti artists who covered sidewalks, monuments, and the walls of buildings with brilliantly comic insults to the Third Reich. Frenchy's best friend had been exe-cuted in the street after being caught painting a Cross of Lorraine on the door of Gestapo headquarters.

"It's a terrible, terrible thing, this war," Frenchy said,

as if it were still going on. "But it gives a man his purpose." His eyes would get misty with scenes of heart-wrenching sadness as he spoke. "Your friends die in your arms, and it is very, very sad. But all the time you know in your heart that their purpose still lives and that they *were* their purpose. A man, Bernard, is not a man unless he is also a purpose. Do you comprehend this, my young friend?"

I nodded soberly, but he was over my head.

"Without a purpose, a man can be dismayed by war. War can drown the spirit of a purposeless man."

I was grateful to him for telling me about the war. He had seen things that were just as terrible as the things my father had seen but they hadn't turned him into a silent brooder. Of course this was ten years after the war had ended and for all I knew my father was able by then to tell stories of the war with equal enthusiasm to some willing listener somewhere in the world.

"Do you understand how important it is to preserve your dignity, Bernard?" Frenchy said to me once. He was visiting Mother and we had just polished off a set of steaks that had cost her a week's worth of tips.

"Sure," I said, but as it always was with Frenchy, this was only his way of opening up a deeper subject.

"It is a ludicrous thing, really. Dignity. Why do we insist on it? In the end, none of us have it. In the end, we are a few ounces of humble dust." His rings and diamond cuff links winked richly in the candlelight.

"And yet, without dignity, life becomes a monstrous slaughterhouse pageant without meaning."

"Let's change the subject," Mother said, pouring coffee.

"No matter what the enemy does to you, Bernard," he said, ignoring her, "you must refuse to submit. His techniques may be subtle, and you may be tempted to bend to his arguments, but you must hold yourself apart from him. Deep within you there is the unviolated place of refusal. You must preserve this, under torture, under bribery, under his vile promises."

"Jesus," Mother said from the kitchen.

"I tell you, my young friend," Frenchy said. "Many many went along with the *boche*. Women and men. They licked the boot."

I was very impressed with Frenchy Bigelow. I told Mother this while we were doing the dishes later that evening. We still had on our good clothes and were both wearing aprons.

After listening to me praise Frenchy, Mother said, "Oh, honey, Frenchy's an old liar. He's never been to France. He's from Detroit. He worked on a GM assembly line during the war."

I found myself rising to his defense. "So *what* if he's lying," I said, "as long as what he's saying is *true.*"

She shut off the water tap and looked at me, drying her hands on her apron. "Listen to yourself, Bernard," she said, mournfully, as if I had just proved beyond doubt that my early promise had been the biggest mis-

37

calculation of her life. "Just listen to what you're saying, Bernard."

But even though Frenchy was a liar, Mother married him a year later anyway. He was as close to rich as she'd seen and money had always been a problem for us after my father left home. I don't think she loved Frenchy in any kind of torch song way, but she got along with him well enough. Frenchy was kind and generous to Woodrow and me, and in return we were a faithful audience for his fabricated tales of life in the French Resistance.

38

In 1958 the draft caught up with Elvis Presley but I was safely enrolled in college by then. I got my 2-S deferment by majoring in electrical engineering. In any future war, I would be stationed, on the grounds of my valuable technical education, well behind the front lines. It was clear, even then, that the gun fodder for future wars would come from the marginally educated legions of aimless young males a society such as ours produces with almost conscious intent. After I graduated, I married the third girl I'd slept with, Beatrice Carns. I got a good job at Lockheed in the industrial town of Sunnyvale, just north of San Jose. A year later, my little brother Woodrow joined the marines and they sent him to officer candidate school.

Lockheed was the prime contractor for a submarine-launched ballistic missile called the Polaris. I worked in a unit that investigated quality control problems with parts and equipment that were supplied to us by sub-

contractors around the country. I traveled a lot, sometimes even to Europe. It was an interesting, even ex-
citing job, but Beatrice became unhappy. She didn't
like it when I was gone, and she didn't seem all that
happy when I was home. We had spontaneous fights
that became the talk of our neighborhood. Beatrice had
a loud voice that carried well down the pleasant tree-
lined street we lived on. I threw chairs and sometimes
overturned tables. Once I drove out of the garage without first opening the door. In a moment of drunken
candor, I admitted to having an affair with the daughter   39
of a German rocket designer in Huntsville, Alabama.

"You dirty heartless pig," Beatrice said, picking up
our one-year-old daughter as if to shield her from the
evil emanating from my person.

A year after Beatrice left me I fell in love with a girl
who worked in the blueprint library named Inez Pascal.
Inez was almost ten years younger than me but that
didn't seem to make much difference to her. We were
soul mates. We told each other this often. For the first
time in my life I understood what passion was. Inez
was small and intense. She did nothing halfway. We
would go out for lunch and wind up, hours later, playing the slots in Reno, work be damned. Inez had
an apartment overlooking the Lockheed parking lot.
When I was laid off in 1968 after an argument with my
lead engineer over my chronic absenteeism, I moved in
with her. The narrow casement windows of her apartment made it seem like a cell. I spent my days there,

watching soap operas or gazing out at the mammoth parking lot as it emptied or filled during shift changes. Then Inez quit her job in protest over the Vietnam War. *"That* is where the war comes from," she said, pointing a righteous finger at the low gray buildings of Lockheed Missiles and Space.

She joined the peace movement and became more intense than ever. She made trips into Berkeley with her new pacifist friends. She asked me to come along, but I refused.

40

"You're apathetic," she said. In those days the crime of apathy was second only to the napalming of villages.

"No," I said, "I just don't think the nerve center of the war is located in Berkeley." Under my glib words I was mourning her once pyrotechnic passion, now diverted to the cause of sane international relations.

We argued, and the argument escalated until it included United States foreign policy, the American Medical Association, and Billy Graham's influence over Richard Nixon. I finally agreed to go to Berkeley with her once, but I didn't join the march on Sproul Hall. I was thirty pounds overweight, almost thirty years old, and balding. I couldn't see myself tramping along with lean, long-haired kids loaded on pot chanting inflammatory slogans as the lines of bored cops itched in their riot gear. That was no way to end a bad war, or start a good one.

I had a hard time finding another job. Boeing made a tepid offer but the job was in North Dakota and Inez refused to go there. There was no peace movement of any impact or glamour in North Dakota. I finally took a job in a large department store in a Santa Clara Valley mall as a plainclothes security guard. I had no experience but I told the interviewer I'd been a brig guard in the marines. He didn't ask to see evidence of my service. I had a boot camp photo of Woodrow and I was prepared to tell the interviewer it was me, fifty pounds lighter, but he was so happy to have landed someone with real experience in handling security matters that he signed me on without further interrogation. It was the Christmas season. If I did well, he said, my job might last until Easter. It was an easy job. I wore a blue blazer, gray slacks, and carried a can of mace, a walkie-talkie. and a set of handcuffs. I worked in men's clothing and in sporting goods on alternate days. It was a minimum wage job, but they gave me discount privileges.

41

Inez spent Christmas day in the Alameda County jail. I cooked the turkey anyway and ate hot sandwiches out on the steel porch of our apartment. The Lockheed parking lot was full and the windows of the gray buildings thrived with feverish light. It reminded me of something one of Inez's new friends once said. "The satanic mills will never stop unless we the people stop them, even if we have to use our own bodies to clog the gears and wheels." It was a popular sentiment. I asked the boy who said this if he had ever seen someone who'd had his arm caught in a grain auger. "You fail to see the point," he said, dismissing me.

I was becoming, I realized, an object of curiosity

among Inez's friends. One of them once asked me to give him my draft card. He was going to mail a box of them to the attorney general's office in Washington. I told him no. We were sitting on the floor of a luxurious apartment that overlooked the sailboat-speckled bay. It belonged to a professor. Everyone looked at me with expressions ranging from contempt to pity. I said, "I'm 4-A. What's the use? No one's going to draft me." Because I was with Inez I was treated like a dupe of the warlords rather than one of their toadies. "Poor old Bernie misses the point," said the professor.

I received a phone call at work one afternoon a few days after Christmas. The store was having a sale and every department was mobbed. My supervisor said to make it quick, two minutes at most. The call was from one of Inez's friends, a boy named Peter Ordway. We had to yell at each other because there was a lot of background noise at both ends of the line—acid rock on his, milling mobs on mine.

"You're *what?*" I shouted, one hand clamped to my free ear.

"Denver. *In* Denver. Didn't have time to tell you. It all happened so fast. Here, talk to Inez."

"We'll be in D.C. a few weeks, then New York," Inez said, her voice quick with the happy excitement once triggered only by me.

"We? You and Peter?"

"Yes. No. Not just Peter and me. Everyone. We're going to be doing some serious guerrilla theater. As much as the warlords would like to believe it, the revolution is not over."

"Why did you call?" I said.

"Don't sound so gloomy. The world hasn't ended. I forgot it's winter back East. Send me my wool sweaters, will you Bernie?"

"Sure," I said. She gave me an address but I didn't write it down.

Just before closing time that day a deranged man entered sporting goods. He was wearing the top half of a Santa Claus costume. His pants were camouflaged combat fatigues. He didn't have any shoes. He was a big man with a dirty white beard. He stood in an aisle, between the baseball gloves and the saltwater tackle, laughing. He had a grand, Mephistophelean laugh that scared most of our customers out of the department.

43

My mouth went a little dry, but there was enough bitterness in me at that moment to cut fear's paralyzing chemicals. I walked up to him, mace in hand.

"Shut up," I said.

He wagged a negative finger in my face, amused. He was tall enough to look down on me. His sharp blue eyes were dancing with the merriment insanity can sometimes produce. He was benignly attentive to everything before him, like a god well pleased with the material fabrications of his inventive dreams.

I raised the mace can so he could see it plainly. But he laughed again, a deep, booming, stagey laugh. He looked like Lee Marvin—rangy, lean, tough with stringy muscle. I sniffed the air between us for alcohol but I'd been drinking earlier that day myself and I couldn't detect anything.

"Come on, sport," I said. "Let's go, okay? It's almost closing time."

"Use it," said my supervisor, yards away behind the canoes. "Use your mace!"

I didn't want to use it. I hated mace, on principle. The madman turned and walked away from me. He overturned a display of golf clubs. Then he sent a rack of executive dumbbells thumping across the tile floor. I tackled him from behind and we went down, hard.

He was as strong as he looked. I tried to stay on top of him but he lifted me off with a roar and I rolled into a low table stacked with Port-a-Potties. When I got up, I saw him moving with guerrilla stealth, doubled over as if avoiding machine gun fire.

Then he was coming at me with a duckboat oar. I waved a skateboard at him. It was total war, suddenly. My war. A war I wasn't fully prepared to wage.

The slow oar stirred the air above my head. I threw the skateboard over his shoulder. He was a graceful, laughing warrior; I was mired in gloom. His war was happy and mine was not. Then one of his demons nagged at him, complicating his attack. He lowered the oar and scratched his head, bewildered, his laughter slowing to a creaky groan. I took the oar out of his hands and laid it down.

His strength, which had been twice mine, was now miraculously atrophied. I handcuffed him easily. His flimsy wrists came together as though they were reeds. The look in his eye was apologetic and puzzled. He was ashamed of himself. The demon that had interrupted his oar-swinging zeal was sanity. It had returned like a dull oceanic depression, bringing with it overcast skies and a mild, enervating drizzle. It made him civil, ineffective, and circumspect. It made room in his heart for fear.

"I'm sorry," he said, his voice surprisingly high-pitched now. "Something must have happened."

I didn't pursue what that might have been. A lot had happened to all of us. I thought of Woodrow who had been wounded in Vietnam two years earlier and had returned home a crazed junky. After committing an exotic sexual crime, he spent a year in the mental hospital at Atascadero. Then he went to Holland. He figured Amsterdam was a good place to be a junky and whatever else he was in the process of becoming. I thought of my father who had gone to the last good war but had returned from it empty, having suffered grievous ruptures to the soul's delicate vessel. I thought of Mother, making her bitter way as a sort of home-front camp follower, the question of dignity postponed for the duration, her calculating eyes fixed to a change-less goal—our survival. Frenchy Bigelow, who had built a cloudy fortress of lies against the daily invasions of conscience, never saw her long-range strategies, or the fierce tenacity that made them work. He believed he was simply and happily married to a worthy, hard-headed woman who allowed him when the profits of Chez Frenchy merited it, small interludes of rest and affection.

And my Inez. She had harnessed her explosive, all-

45

out passion to the ready yoke of righteousness. After her sorties to Washington and New York, and later to Bonn and Brussels, she would have no use at all for doubtful heroes like me who would never fight for the cause of the moment—unless they were caught in its feverish arms and *combat* was the only way out of that sweaty embrace.

My prisoner sat on a stool in the supervisor's office waiting for the police. I sat with him, chain-smoking. Burdened by sanity, we both cast nervous, self-conscious glances at the big clock on the wall.

The Smile of a Turtle

COBB KNOWS the cooped housewives need
him. A new breed of degenerate (de-gents, Cobb calls
them) has been making the headlines. A door-to-door
salesman with a sharp yen for the average, haggard,
wide-beam housewife. Cobb saw it in the *Times* yesterday morning. This de-gent peddling a glass knife guaranteed to slice overripe tomatoes. College educated guy
at that. Nice, trim, clean-cut, good suit from Bullock's
or Macy's, and this normally cautious housewife *lets
him in*. He demonstrated his glass knife on her. Sliced
her, diced her, iced her. Then went out to his Volvo to
jerk off. Bad news. The bad old world is full of it,
but Cobb's product promises freedom from such bad
dreams. He holds the three-inch chrome-plated cylin-
der up to the cracked (but still chained) door so that the
lady can see it clearly. His blond, unlined face looks
harmless and sincere and deeply concerned about
Home Security. It's his business, and Cobb has been
working the hot neighborhoods of West L.A. all morning this burning day in early August.

"You need this device, ma'am," Cobb says, sincere as the Eagle Scout he once was. "Every housewife in L.A. needs it. A simple demonstration will make this abundantly clear. The de-gents, ma'am, are everywhere." He says "ma'am" in the soft southern way to slow her trotting heart. But the gadget sells itself. And it's a bargain at five dollars. Ten would be fair and most would pay twenty, but all he wants is the price of a movie ticket. Isn't home security worth at least that much— the price of, say, *Friday the 13th Part Three* or *Dressed to Kill?*

50

She opens the door a hair wider, hooked. Cobb looks like her kid brother, or her old high school boyfriend, or maybe the nice boy who delivers the paper. All-American Cleancut. He looks harmless as a puppy. There's even something cuddly about him, something you could *pet.* A dancing prickle of heat glides across the nape of her neck and into her hair line.

Cobb is working on projecting these positive vibes. He feels that he's able, now, to radiate serious alpha waves. His boss, Jake the Distributor, has this theory. He thinks every man and woman is an animal at heart. We respond, he says, to the animal in each other. We see it in our little unconscious moves and gestures. We see it in our eyes. The trick, says Jake the Distributor, is to identify *your* personal animal and let the pure alpha waves flow out of it. This is how you become your proper self. This is how you become a world-class salesman. Jake the Distributor has studied the subject in depth. "You," he said to Cobb, "are obviously a turtle."

He said this at a big sales meeting and everyone laughed. Turtle, what good is a turtle, Cobb thought, humiliated, and, as if answering his thoughts, someone hollered, "Soup! Soup!" and they all laughed at him and among the laughers he identified the barking hyenas and dogs, the hooting chimps and gibbons, and the softly hissing turtles.

Cobb bought Jake the Distributor's theory. He made a study of turtles. The Chinese had some definite ideas about them, for instance. On the plus side, turtles are careful and shy, fond of warm mud, and ready to leave a bad scene at the first sign of trouble. On the minus side, they are shifty, shiftless, and dirty-minded. They think about getting it morning, noon, and night. They are *built* for getting it. Even their tails help out. The turtle tail is prehensile during the act. It holds the female close and tight and there's no way she can detach herself once things get under way. Turtles can screw ten, fifteen times a day and not lose interest.

But Jake the Distributor says, Emphasize the positive and you will make your fortune. Keep your fingernails clean and clipped. Wash up several times a day—you can develop a bad stink walking the neighborhoods all day long. Change your shorts. Use a strong underarm spray. Don't touch yourself out of habit in the area of your privates while in the process of making a pitch. Keep a good shine on your shoes. Keep your nap up. Hair trimmed and combed. Teeth white, breath sweet, pits dry. Groom, groom, groom.

It's the brace-and-bit, though, that tends to do ma-

51

jor harm to his first good impression. This can't be helped—tools of the trade. Cobb tries to hold it down behind his leg. But she's seen it and is holding her breath. So he starts his pitch, talking fast. "It's called Cyclops, ma'am," he says. (Southern, says Jake the Distributor, don't forget to sound southern. They *trust* southern. Sound New York and you are dead meat in the street. Sound L.A. and you get no pay. Think genteel, southern Mississippi. Think graceful Georgia. But do not think Okie. Talk Okie and they will pee their drawers. Bike gangs are Okie. Bible salesmen are weirdo Okie. Think magnolia blossoms and mint juleps. Think *Gone With the Wind*. Make them think they are Scarlett O'Hara.) "The *Farrago* Cyclops, ma'am," Cobb explains. "Charles V. Farrago being the name of the gentleman who invented it and who currently holds the exclusive manufacturing rights. Yes, there are many cheap imitations, ma'am, but there is only one Farrago Cyclops!"

She stands there blinking in the crack of the chained door. She's a *mouse,* Cobb begins to realize. Thirty-five to forty, afraid of sudden moves and noise, bright outdoor light always a threat, for there are hawks, there are cats. Her house is dark inside, like a cave chewed into wood by quick, small teeth. She is wearing a gray housecoat and she is nibbling something—a piece of cheese!—and Cobb almost grins in her face, pleased that he's identified her secret animal so perfectly.

He fights back his knowing smile, for the smile of a turtle is a philosophical thing. It tends to put things into

52

long-term perspective. It makes the recipient think: there's more to this situation than I presently understand. It will give the recipient a chill. A mouse will run from such a smile, though in nature mice and turtles are not enemies. But, Cobb thinks, we are not in nature. This is L.A., this is the world. He masters the smile and muscles it back to where it came from.

"Here you go, ma'am," he says. "Take it. Try it." She receives it gingerly, as if it were a loaded gun with a hair trigger. *Microtus pennsylvanicus,* Cobb thinks, mouse, and that is what she surely was meant to be, down to the cream cheese marrow of her small bones. He begins to think of her as "Minnie."

53

Cobb kneels down suddenly on her welcome mat. Stitched into a sisal mat are the letters of a Spanish word, *bienvenido.* He crouches down as low as he can get. Neighborhood children freeze with curiosity on their skateboards. The heat leans down through the perpetually grainy sky. In the north, the annual arsonists have set fire to the brushy hills once again. In the east, flash floods. Rapists, stranglers, and slashers roam the jammed tract-house valleys. Santa Ana wind, moaning in the TV antennas, spills over the mountains from the desert, electrifying the air. The ionized air lays a charge on the surface of his skin, the hair of his arms stands up stiff and surly, as if muscled, and his brain feels tacked into its casing. His back is soaked with sweat and his pits are swampy.

"Sometimes these de-gents will ring the bell, ma'am," he says, "and then drop down to all fours like this, hoping that the lady occupant, such as yourself, will make the fatal mistake of opening the door to see what's going on even though she didn't see anybody in the peephole. Some of these de-gents are real weasels, take my word for it. But the Farrago Cyclops will expose them, due to the fish-eye lens system." And he can see now that she is suddenly gripped by the idea of the sort of *weasel* who would ring her bell and then hide on the doorstep, waiting to spring.

"The worst is sure to happen, ma'am," he says gravely, "sooner or later, because of the nature of the perverted mind in today's world. This is a proven fact, known to most as Murphy's Law." Cobb makes a movement with his wrist, suggesting a weapon. Sledge, ax, awl, ice pick, the rapist's long razor. He shows her some crotch bulge, the possible avenger in there, coiled to strike. "You *can* see me, ma'am?" he asks. She gives one nod, her face crimped up as she peers into the Cyclops. "That's it, ma'am," says Cobb, doing Georgia, doing 'Bama. "Hold it level to the ground, as if it was already in place in your door."

"You sort of look funny," she says. "Oblong. Or top-heavy."

"It's the lens, ma'am. Fish eye. It puts a bend in the world, but you get to see more of it that way."

Cobb stands up and makes a quick pencil mark on the door. "Right about here, I guess. What are you, ma'am, about five foot one?" She nods. "Husband gone most of the day? His work take him out of town a lot?" She looks like a fading photograph of herself.

Cobb stops his grin before it crawls into his lips. He raises the brace-and-bit, pauses just long enough to get her consent, which she gives by stepping backward a few inches and turning her head slightly to one side, a gesture of acquiescence, and Cobb scores the flimsy laminated wood with the tip of the bit and starts the hole, one inch in diameter, right on the pencil mark, level with her wide open eyes. He leans on the brace and cranks. The wood is tract-house cheap, false-grain oak, so thin that a child of nine could kick a hole in it.

To see how fast her door can be penetrated unsettles her and so Cobb tries to calm her down with a brief outline of the Charles V. Farrago success story. Rags to riches in the Home Security field. From shop mechanic to multimillionaire. From Cedar Rapids to Carmel by the Sea. The undisputed king of home surveillance devices. A genius by any standard. Cobb carries a photograph of Charles V. Farrago and promises to show it to the woman as soon as he drills out her door. In the photograph, taken some twenty or thirty years ago, Farrago has a big round head and a smile that seems two hands across with more teeth in it than seem possible. He has shrewd little eyes that preside above the smile like twin watchdogs.

Cobb tells the woman other stories. He tells her about the woman, housewife like herself, who had oil of vitriol pumped up her nose through one of those old fashioned door-peepers. Knock knock, and she opened the little peeper to see who was there and it was a degent. Splat. Blinded for life and horribly disfigured all

55

for the want of a proper doorstep surveillance device. Blue crater where once was her nose, upper lip a leather flap, eyes milky clouds. The reason? No *reason*. There never is a reason. It was a prank. The de-gent chemistry student had seen *Phantom of the Opera* on TV. It was Halloween in Denver or Salt Lake or Omaha. A few years ago. He told the police: "I just had this big urge to melt a face, you know?"

Cobb tells her the one about the naked de-gent who knocked on a peeperless door and said, "Parcel Post!" He made love to his victim with a gardening tool right in front of her little kids. He left a red hoofprint on her shag carpet and that's how the cops caught him: his right foot only had two toes and the print looked like it had been left there by a goat. The *Times* called him "The Goatfoot Gasher."

The grumbling bit chews through the last lamination of veneer and Cobb reaches around the still-chained door to catch the curls of blond wood which he puts into his shirt pocket. Do not leave an unsightly mess, says Jake the Distributor. Be neat as a pin. Cobb inserts the Cyclops gently and with a little sigh into the tight hole then screws on the locking flange. "Let's give it a try, ma'am," he says.

She closes the door and Cobb goes out to the sidewalk. He stands still long enough for her to get used to the odd shapes the fish-eye lens produces, then starts to move down the sidewalk in big sidesteps. Then he reverses direction, moving in sidesteps to the other extreme of her vision. He approaches the house on the

56

oblique, crossing the lawn, dropping behind a shrub, reemerging on hands and knees, moving swiftly now like a Dirty Dozen commando toward the welcome mat. He knows what she is seeing, knows how the lens makes him look heavy through the middle, pin-headed, legs stubby, his shined shoes fat as seals, the mean unsmiling lips, the stumpy bulge at the apex of his fat thighs, the neighborhood curving around him like a psychopathic smirk.

"It really works," she says, showing as much enthu-siasm as she feels she can afford when Cobb reappears at the door, brushing off his knees and smiling like a helpful Scout. She slips a five-dollar bill through the cracked door and Cobb notices that it has been folded into a perfect square the size of a stamp.

"Satisfaction fully guaranteed, ma'am," he says, unfolding, meticulously, the bill. A fragrance, trapped in the bill for possibly years, makes his nostrils flare.

Cobb winks and the woman allows herself a coo of gratitude. Turtle and mouse rapport, Cobb thinks, pleased. This is what you strive for, says Jake the Dis-tributor. Cross the species lines. This is the hallmark of the true salesman. Make them think you are just like them, practically *kin,* though we know that this is basi-cally laughable.

This is Cobb's tenth sale this morning. He keeps one dollar and fifteen cents out of every five. On good days he'll sell fifty. But today won't be a good day—for sales, at least. Too hot. He feels as if there's this big unfair hand in the sky that's been lowering all morning, pushing him down. He needs a break. He needs to cool off, wash up—a nice shower would do it—he needs to get out of his swampy shirt, air his pits and the steaming crotch of his slacks. He wants to use her john, but he knows her mouse heart will panic if he asks. Instead, he asks if he can use her phone. "Need to check in," he explains, his voice decent, a fellow human being making a reasonable request, a finely honed act. She fades a bit, but she is not a swift thinker and can't find a way to say no pleasantly. Cobb has his Eagle Scout glow turned up full blast. His boylike vulnerability is apparent in the bend of his spine, put there by the unfair bone-warping hand that presses down on him from the dirty sky, trying to make him crawl again, but he is through crawling today and is ready to lay claim to the small things of this world that should be his, but are not. The woman slides the chained bolt out of its slot and opens the door wide in jerky, indecisive increments.

"Oh, lady," he says, his voice relaxing now into its natural cadence. "You're the angel of mercy in the flesh. Really." And Cobb, hard thin lips flexed in a triumphant V, walks in.

A BLACK HELICOPTER flapped out of the morning sun and dumped its sweet orange mist on our land instead of the Parley farm where it was intended. It was weedkiller, something strong enough to wipe out leafy spurge, knapweed and Canadian thistle, but it made us sick.

My father had a fatal stroke a week after that first spraying. I couldn't hold down solid food for nearly a month and went from 200 pounds to 170 in that time. Mama went to bed and slept for two days, and when she woke up she was not the same. She'd lost something of herself in that long sleep, and something that wasn't herself had replaced it.

Then it hit the animals. We didn't have much in the way of animals, but one by one they dropped. The chickens, the geese, the two old mules—Doc and Rex— and last of all, our only cow, Miss Milky, who was more or less the family pet.

Miss Milky was the only animal that didn't outright up and die. She just got sick. There was blood in her milk and her milk was thin. Her teats got so tender and brittle that she would try to mash me against the milk stall wall when I pulled at them. The white part of her eyes looked like fresh red meat. Her piss was so strong that the green grass wherever she stood died off. She got so bound up that when she'd lift her tail and bend with strain, only one black apple would drop. Her breath took on a burning sulphurous stink that would make you step back.

62 She also went crazy. She'd stare at me like she all at once had a desperate human mind and had never seen me before. Then she'd act as if she wanted to slip a horn under my ribs and peg me to the barn. She would drop her head and charge, blowing like a randy bull, and I would have to scramble out of the way. Several times I saw her gnaw on her hooves or stand stock-still in water up to her blistered teats. Or she would walk backward all day long, mewling like a lost cat that had been dropped off in a strange place. That mewling was enough to make you want to clap a set of noise dampers on your ears. The awful sound led Mama to say this: "It's the death song of the land, mark my words."

Mama never talked like that before in her life. She'd always been a cheerful woman who could never see the bad part of anything that was at least fifty percent good. But now she was dark and strange as a gypsy, and she would have spells of sheer derangement during which she'd make noises like a wild animal, or she'd play the part of another person—the sort of person she'd normally have nothing to do with at all. At

Daddy's funeral, she got dressed up in an old and tattered evening gown the color of beet juice, her face painted and powdered like that of a barfly. And while the preacher told the onlookers what a fine man Daddy had been, Mama cupped her hands under her breasts and lifted them high, as if offering to appease a dangerous stranger. Then, ducking her head, she chortled, "Loo, loo, loo," her scared eyes scanning the trees for owls.

I was twenty-eight years old and my life had come to nothing. I'd had a girl but I'd lost her through neglect and a careless attitude that had spilled over into my personal life, souring it. I had no ambition to make something worthwhile of myself, and it nettled her. Toward the end, she began to parrot her mother: "You need to get yourself *established,* Jack," she would say. But I didn't want to get myself established. I was getting poorer and more aimless day by day, and I supposed she believed that "getting established" would put a stop to the downhill slide, but I had no desire to do whatever it took to accomplish that.

Shortly after Daddy died, the tax man came to our door with a paper in his hand. "Inheritance tax," he said, handing me the paper.

"What do you mean?" I asked.

"It's the law," he said. "Your father died, you see. And that's going to cost you some. You should have made better plans." He tapped his forehead with his finger and winked. He had a way of expressing himself that made me think he was country born and raised but wanted to seem citified. Or maybe it was the other way around.

"I don't understand this," I mumbled. I felt the weight of a world I'd so far been able to avoid. It was out there, tight-assed and squinty-eyed, and it knew to the dollar and dime what it needed to keep itself in business.

"Simple," he said. "Pay or move off. The government is the government, and it can't bend a rule to accommodate the confused. It's your decision. Pay or the next step is litigation."

He smiled when he said good-bye. I closed the door against the weight of his smile, which was the weight of the world. I went to a window and watched him head back to his green government car. The window was open and I could hear him. He was singing loudly in a fine tenor voice. He raised his right hand to hush an invisible audience that had broken into uncontrolled applause. I could still hear him singing as he slipped the car into gear and idled away. He was singing "Red River Valley."

Even though the farm was all ours, paid up in full, we had to give the government $7,000 for the right to stay on it. The singing tax man said we had inherited the land from my father, and the law was sharp on the subject.

I didn't know where the money was going to come from. I didn't talk it over with Mama because even in her better moments she would talk in riddles. To a

64

simple question such as, "Should I paint the barns this year, Mama?" she might answer, "I've no eyes for glitter, nor ears for their ridicule."

One day I decided to load Miss Milky into the stock trailer and haul her into Saddle Butte where the vet, Doc Nevers, had his office. Normally, Doc Nevers would come out to your place, but he'd heard about the spraying that was going on and said he wouldn't come within three miles of our property until they were done.

The Parley farm was being sprayed regularly, for they grew an awful lot of wheat and almost as much corn, and they had the biggest haying operation in the county. Often, the helicopters they used were upwind from us and we were sprayed too. ("Don't complain," said Big Pete Parley when I called him up about it. "Think of it this way—you're getting your place weeded for *free!*" When I said I might have to dynamite some stumps on the property line and that he might get a barn or two blown away for free, he just laughed like hell, as if I had told one of the funniest jokes he'd ever heard.)

There was a good windbreak between our places, a thick grove of lombardy poplars, but the orange mist, sweet as a flower garden in full bloom, sifted through the trees and settled on our fields. Soon the poplars were mottled and dying. Some branches curled in an upward twist, as if flexed in pain, and others became soft and fibrous as if the wood were trying to turn itself into sponge.

65

With Miss Milky in the trailer, I sat in the truck sipping on a pint of Lewis and Clark bourbon and looking out across our unplanted fields. It was late—almost too late—to plant anything. Mama, in the state she was in, hadn't even noticed.

In the low hills on the north side of the property, some ugly looking things were growing. From the truck, they looked like white pimples on the smooth brown hill. Up close, they were big as melons. They were some kind of fungus, and they pushed up through the ground like the bald heads of fat babies. They gave off a rotten meat stink. I would get chillbumps just looking at them, and if I touched one, my stomach would rise. The bulbous heads had purple streaks on them that looked like blood vessels. I half expected to one day see human eyes clear the dirt and open. Big pale eyes that would see me and carry my image down to their deepest root. I was glad they seemed to prefer the hillside and bench and not the bottom land.

Justified or not, I blamed the growth of this fungus on the poison spray, just as I blamed it for the death of my father, the loss of our animals, and the strangeness of my mother. Now the land itself was becoming strange. And I thought, what about me? How am I being rearranged by that weedkiller?

I guess I should have gotten mad, but I didn't. Maybe I *had* been changed by the spray. Where once I had been a quick-to-take-offense hothead, I was now docile and thoughtful. I could sit on a stump and think for hours, enjoying the slow and complicated intertwinings of my own thoughts. Even though I felt sure the cause of all our troubles had fallen out of the sky, I would hold arguments with myself, as if there were always two sides to every question. If I said to myself, "Big Pete Parley has poisoned my family and farm and my father is dead because of it," I would follow it up with, "But Daddy was old anyway, past seventy-five, and he always had high blood pressure. Anything could have set off his stroke, from a wasp bite to a sonic boom."

"And what about Mama?" I would ask. "Senile   67 with grief," came the quick answer. "Furthermore, Daddy himself used poison in his time. Cyanide traps for coyotes, DDT for mosquito larvae, arsenic for rats."

My mind was always doubling back on itself in this way, and it would often leave me standing motionless in a field for hours, paralyzed with indecision, sighing like a moonstruck girl of twelve. I imagined myself mistaken by passersby for a scarecrow.

Sometimes I saw myself as a human weed, useless to other people in general and maybe harmful in some weedy way. The notion wasn't entirely unpleasant. Jack Hucklebone: a weed among the well-established money crops of life.

On my way to town with Miss Milky, I crossed over the irrigation ditch my father had fallen into with the stroke that killed him. I pulled over onto the shoulder and switched off the engine. It was a warm, insect-loud day in early June. A spray of grasshoppers clattered over the hood of the truck. June bugs ticked past the windows like little flying clocks. The thirteen-year locusts were back and raising a whirring hell. I was fifteen the last time they came, but I didn't remember them arriving in such numbers. I expected more helicopters to come flapping over with special sprays meant just for them, even though they would be around for only a few weeks and the damage they would do is not much more than measurable. But anything that looks like it might have an appetite for a money crop brings down the spraying choppers. I climbed out of the truck and looked up into the bright air. A lone jet, eastbound, too high to see or hear, left its neat chalk line across the top of the sky. The sky itself was like hot blue wax, north to south. A giant hammerhead sat on the west horizon as if it were a creamy oblong planet gone dangerously off-course.

68

There's where Daddy died. Up the ditch about fifty yards from here. I found him, buckled, white as paper, half under water. His one good eye, his right (he'd lost the left one thirty years ago when a tractor tire blew up in his face as he was filling it), was above water and wide open, staring at his hand as if it could focus on the thing it gripped. He was holding on to a root. He had big hands, strong, with fingers like thick hardwood dowels, but now they were soft and puffy, like the hands of a giant baby. Water bugs raced against the current toward him. His body blocked the ditch and little eddies swirled around it. The water bugs skated into the eddies and, fighting to hold themselves still in the roiling current, touched his face. They held still long enough to satisfy their curiosity, then slid back into the circular flow as if bemused by the strangeness of dead human flesh.

I started to cry, remembering it, thinking about him in the water, he had been so sure and strong, but then—true to my changed nature—I began to laugh at the memory, for his wide blue eye had had a puzzled cast to it, as if it had never before seen such a crazy thing as the ordinary root in his forceless hand. It was an expression he never wore in life.

"It was only a weed, Daddy," I said, wiping the tears from my face.

The amazed puzzlement stayed in his eye until I brushed down the lid.

Of course he had been dead beyond all talk and puzzlement. Dead when I found him, dead for hours, bloated dead. And this is how *I've* come to be—blame the spray or don't: the chores don't get done on time, the unplanted fields wait, Mama wanders in her mind, and yet I'll sit in the shade of my truck sipping on Lewis and Clark bourbon, inventing the thoughts of a stone-dead man.

Time bent away from me like a tail-dancing rainbow. It was about to slip the hook. I wasn't trying to hold it. Try to hold it and it gets all the more slippery. Try to let it go and it sticks like a cocklebur to cotton. I was drifting somewhere between the two kinds of not trying: not trying to hold anything, not trying to let anything go.

69

Then he sat down next to me. The old man.

"You got something for me?" he said.

He was easily the homeliest man I had ever seen. His bald head was bullet-shaped and his lumpy nose was warty as a crookneck squash. His little, close-set eyes sat on either side of that nose like hard black beans. He had shaggy eyebrows that climbed upward in a white and wiry tangle. There was a blue lump in the middle of his forehead the size of a pullet's egg, and his hairy ear lobes touched his grimy collar. He was mumbling something, but it could have been the noise of the ditch water as it sluiced through the culvert under the road.

He stank of whiskey and dung, and looked like he'd been sleeping behind barns for weeks. His clothes were rags, and he was caked with dirt from fingernail to jaw. His shoes were held together with strips of burlap. He untied some of these strips and took off the shoes. Then he slid his gnarled, dirt-crusted feet into the water. His eyes fluttered shut and he let out a hissing moan of pleasure. His toes were long and twisted, the arthritic knuckles painfully bright. They reminded me of the surface roots of a stunted oak that had been trying to grow in hardpan. Though he was only about five feet tall, his feet were huge. Easy size twelves, wide as paddles.

He quit mumbling, cleared his throat, spit. "You got something for me?" he said.

I handed him my pint. He took it, then held it up to the sunlight and looked through the rusty booze as if testing for its quality.

"If it won't do," I said, "I could run into town to get

70

something a little smoother for you. Maybe you'd like some Canadian Club or some twelve-year-old Scotch. I could run into town and be back in less than an hour. Maybe you'd like me to bring back a couple of fried chickens and a sack of buttered rolls." This was my old self talking, the hothead. But I didn't feel mad at him, and was just being mouthy out of habit.

"No need to do that," he said, as if my offer had been made in seriousness. He took a long pull off my pint. "This snake piss is just fine by me, son." He raised the bottle to the sunlight again, squinted through it.

I wandered down the ditch again to the place where Daddy died. There was nothing there to suggest a recent dead man had blocked the current. Everything was as it always was. The water surged, the quick water bugs skated up and down, inspecting brown clumps of algae along the banks; underwater weeds waved like slim snakes whose tails had been staked to the mud. I looked for the thistle he'd grabbed on to. I guess he thought that he was going to save himself from drowning by hanging on to its root, not realizing that the killing flood was *inside* his head. But there were many roots along the bank and none of them seemed more special than any other.

Something silver glinted at me. It was a coin. I picked it out of the slime and polished it against my pants. It was a silver dollar, a real one. It could have been his. He carried a few of the old cartwheels around with him for luck. The heft and gleam of the old solid silver coin choked me up.

I walked back to the old man. He had stuffed his

71

bindle under his head for a pillow and had dozed off. I uncapped the pint and finished it, then flipped it into the weeds. It hit a rock and popped. The old man grunted and his eyes snapped open. He let out a barking snort, and his black eyes darted around him fiercely, like the eyes of a burrow animal caught in a daylight trap. Then, remembering where he was, he calmed down.

"You got something for me?" he asked. He pushed himself up to a sitting position. It was a struggle for him.

72   "Not any more," I said. I sat down next to him. Then, from behind us, a deep groan cut loose. It sounded like siding being pried off an old barn with a crowbar. We both turned to look at whatever had complained so mightily.

It was Miss Milky, up in the trailer, venting her misery. I'd forgotten about her. Horseflies were biting her. Her red eyes peered sadly out at us through the bars. The corners of her eyes were swollen, giving her a Chinese look.

With no warning at all, a snapping hail fell on us. Only it wasn't hail. It was a moving cloud of thirteen-year locusts. They darkened the air and they covered us. The noise was like static on the radio, miles of static across the bug-peppered sky, static that could drown out all important talk and idle music, no matter how powerful the station.

The old man's face was covered with the bugs and he was saying something to me, but I couldn't make out what it was. His mouth opened and closed, opened and closed. When it opened, he'd have to brush away the locusts from his lips. They were like ordinary grasshoppers, only smaller, and they had big red eyes that seemed to glow with their own hellish light. Then, as fast as they had come, they were gone, scattered back into the fields. A few hopped here and there, but the main cloud had broken up.

I just sat there, brushing at the lingering feel of them on my skin and trying to readjust myself to uncluttered air, but my ears were still crackling with their racket.

The old man pulled at my sleeve, breaking me out of my daydream or trance. "You got something for me?" he asked.

I felt blue. Worse than blue. Sick. I felt incurable— ridden with the pointlessness of just about everything you could name. The farm struck me as a pointless wonder, and I found the idea depressing and fearsome. Pointless bugs lay waiting in the fields for the pointless crops as the pointless days and seasons ran on and on into the pointless forever.

"Shit," I said.

"I'll take that worthless cow off your hands, then," said the old man. "She's done for. All you have to do is look at her."

"No shit," I said.

He didn't seem so old or so wrecked to me now. He was younger and bigger, somehow, as if all his clocks had started spinning backwards, triggered by the locust cloud. He stood up. He looked thick across the shoulders like he'd done hard work all his life and could still do it. He showed me his right hand and it was yellow with hard calluses. His beady black eyes were quick and lively in their shallow sockets. The blue lump on his forehead glinted in the sun. It seemed deliberately polished, as if it were an ornament. He took a little silver bell out of his pocket and rang it for no reason at all.

"Let me have her," he said.

"You want Miss Milky?" I asked. I felt weak and childish. Maybe I was drunk. My scalp itched and I scratched it hard. He rang his little silver bell again. I wanted to have it, but he put it back into his pocket. Then he knelt down and opened his bindle. He took out a paper sack.

I looked inside. It was packed with seeds of some kind. I ran my fingers through them and did not feel foolish. I heard a helicopter putt-putting in the distance. In defense of what I did, let me say this much: I knew Miss Milky was done for. Doc Nevers would have told me to kill her. I don't think she was even good for hamburger. Old cow meat can sometimes make good hamburger, but Miss Milky looked wormy and lean. And I wouldn't have trusted her bones for soup. The poison that had wasted her flesh and ruined her udder had probably settled in her marrow.

And so I unloaded my dying cow. He took out his silver bell again and tied it to a piece of string. He tied the string around Miss Milky's neck. Then he led her away. She was docile and easy, as though this was exactly the way things were supposed to turn out.

My throat was dry. I felt too tired to move. I watched their slow progress down the path that ran along the ditch. They got smaller and smaller in the field until, against a dark hedge of box elders, they disappeared. I strained to see after them, but it was as if the earth had given them refuge, swallowing them into its deep, loamy, composting interior. The only sign that they still existed in the world was the tinkling of the silver bell he had tied around Miss Milky's neck. It was a pure sound, naked on the air.

Then a breeze opened a gap in the box elders and a long blade of sunlight pierced through them, illuminating and magnifying the old man and his cow, as if the air between us had formed itself into a giant lens. The breeze let up and the box elders shut off the sun again, and I couldn't see anything but a dense quiltwork of black and green shadows out of which a raven big as an eagle flapped. It cawed in raucous good humor as it veered over my head.

75

I went on into town anyway, cow or no cow, and hit some bars. I met a girl from the East in the Hobble who thought I was a cowboy and I didn't try to correct her mistaken impression, for it proved to be a free pass to good times.

When I got home, Mama had company. She was dressed up in her beet juice gown, and her face was powdered white. Her dark lips looked like a wine stain in snow. But her clear blue eyes were direct and calm. There was no distraction in them.

"Hi boy," said the visitor. It was Big Pete Parley. He was wearing a blue suit, new boots, a gray felt Stetson. He had a toothy grin on his fat red face.

I looked at Mama. "What's *he* want?" I asked.

"Mr. Parley is going to help us, Jackie," she said.

"What's going on, Mama?" I asked. Something was wrong. I could feel it but I couldn't see it. It was Mama, the way she was carrying herself maybe, or the look in her eyes and her whitened skin. Maybe she had gone all the way insane. She went over to Parley and sat next to him on the davenport. She had slit her gown and it fell away from her thigh, revealing the veiny flesh.

"We're going to be married," she said. "Pete's tired of being a widower. He wants a warm bed."

As if to confirm it was no fantasy dreamed up by her senile mind, Big Pete slipped his meaty hand into the slit dress and squeezed her thigh. He clicked his teeth and winked at me.

"Pete knows how to operate a farm," said Mama. "And you do not, Jackie." She didn't intend for it to sound mean or critical. It was just a statement of the way things were. I couldn't argue with her.

I went into the kitchen. Mama followed me in. I opened a beer. "I don't mean to hurt your feelings, Jackie," she said.

"He's scheming to get our land," I said. "He owns half the county, but it isn't enough."

"No," she said. "I'm the one who's scheming. I'm scheming for my boy who does not grasp the rudiments of the world."

I had the sack of seeds with me. I realized that I'd been rattling them nervously.

"What do you have there?" she asked, narrowing her eyes.

"Seeds," I said.

"Seeds? What seeds? Who gave you seeds? Where'd you get them?"

I thought it best not to mention where I'd gotten them. "Big Pete Parley doesn't want to marry *you*," I said. It was a mean thing to say, and I wanted to say it.

Mama sighed. "It doesn't matter what he wants, Jack. I'm dead anyway." She took the bag of seeds from me, picked some up, squinted at them.

"What is that supposed to mean?" I said, sarcastically.

She went to the window above the sink and stared out into the dark. Under the folds of her evening gown, I could see the ruined shape of her old body. "Dead, Jack," she said. "I've been dead for a while now. Maybe you didn't notice."

"No," I said. "I didn't."

"Well, you should have. I went to sleep shortly after your Daddy died and I had a dream. The dream got stronger and stronger as it went on until it was as vivid as real life itself. More vivid. When I woke up I knew that I had died. I also knew that nothing in the world would ever be as real to me as that dream."

I almost asked her what the dream was about, but I didn't, out of meanness. In the living room Big Pete

77

Parley was whistling impatiently. The davenport was squeaking under his nervous weight.

"So, you see, Jackie," said Mama. "It doesn't matter if I marry Pete Parley or what his motives are in this matter. You are all that counts now. He will ensure your success in the world."

"I don't want to be a success, Mama," I said.

"Well, you have no choice. You cannot gainsay the dead."

She opened the window and dumped out the sack of seeds. Then Big Pete Parley came into the kitchen. "Let's go for a walk," he said. "It's too blame hot in this house."

They left by the kitchen door. I watched them walk across the yard and into the dark, unplanted field. Big Pete had his arm around Mama's shoulder. I wondered if he knew, or cared, that he was marrying a dead woman. Light from the half-moon painted their silhouettes for a while. Then the dark field absorbed them.

I went to bed and slept for what might have been days. In my long sleep I had a dream. I was canoeing down a whitewater river that ran sharply uphill. The farther up I got, the rougher the water became. Finally, I had to beach the canoe. I proceeded on foot until I came to a large gray house that had been built in a wilderness forest. The house was empty and quiet. I went in. It was clean and beautifully furnished. Nobody was home. I called out a few times before I understood that silence was a rule. I went from room to room, going deeper and deeper toward some dark interior place. I understood that I was involved in a search. The longer I searched, the more vivid the dream became.

When I woke up I was stiff and weak. Mama wasn't in the house. I made a pot of coffee and took a cup outside. Under the kitchen window there was a patch of green shoots that had not been there before. "You got something for me?" I said.

A week later that patch of green shoots had grown and spread. They were weeds. The worst kind of weeds I had ever seen. Thick, spiny weeds, with broad green leaves tough as leather. They rolled away from the house, out across the fields, in a viny carpet. Mean, deep-rooted weeds, too mean to uproot by hand. When I tried, I came away with a palm full of cuts.

In another week they were tall as corn. They were fast growers and I could not see where they ended. They covered everything in sight. A smothering blanket of deep green sucked the life out of every other growing thing. They crossed fences, irrigation ditches, and when they reached the trees of a windbreak, they became ropy crawlers that wrapped themselves around trunks and limbs.

When they reached the Parley farm, over which my dead mother now presided, they were attacked by squadrons of helicopters which drenched them in poisons, the best poisons chemical science knew how to brew. But the poisons only seemed to make the weeds grow faster, and after a spraying the new growths were

79

tougher, thornier, and more determined than ever to dominate the land.

Some of the weeds sent up long woody stalks. On top of these stalks were heavy seedpods, fat as melons. The strong stalks pushed the pods high into the air.

The day the pods cracked, a heavy wind came up. The wind raised black clouds of seed in grainy spirals that reached the top of the sky, then scattered them, far and wide, across the entire nation.

Life Between Meals

"DIG IN!" I'd say, and the silverware would fly!
Those were the days. If we saw a nibbler we would always be sure to let him see us unload our heaping forks. Our cheeks would balloon, our nostrils flare, and our eyes would roll with the sheer ecstasy of eating. The nibbler would usually dab his pinched-up mouth with his napkin and wash down his pellet of food with quick sips of water. A sickening tribe of birds, are they not? They make me gag.

We traveled a lot. The first thing we would do in a new town would be to scout the restaurants. And I mean *restaurants.* I do not mean the fast food slop houses, the so-called "coffee shoppes," or the little neighborhood diners where you eat at considerable risk. Ptomaine, I mean. We gave them grades. A for best, F for dismal failure. Quality and *quantity* first, service second. Atmosphere a distant third. We do not eat the atmosphere.

Now hear this: are you nervous? Are you thin? Then *eat!* What do you want to be like that for? Eat, sleep, and move your bowels. This is basic. This is life. I have seen too many human skeletons, *nibblers*, nervous as cats, eating that ghastly jello on lettuce. Their reward? Stubborn stool dry as birdshot, and they sleep in fits.

I speak from experience. I was there. We were thin. "Doctor's orders." Antoinette was down to one hundred and forty pounds, and I teetered at two-twenty. We were a pair of rails. I looked somehow fraudulent in my uniform—no bearing, no authority, no style. A year before I'd been up to three-sixteen and Antoinette was two-oh-nine. We were a hefty duo, and happy. The famous internist said, "You lose one hundred pounds of that lard, Commodore, or you're sunk. Your heart will not bear the strain." And I believed his claptrap.

Broiled slivers of freshwater fish, naked green salads, fruit cocktails sweetened with something made out of coal tar, unsalted wafers, zwieback, fingers of asparagus without a nice blanket of cheese sauce, and, of course, the ever-present jello on lettuce. We went through hell. We suffered. And for what, I ask.

Our health did not noticeably improve. Personally, I felt worse. I believed my death was imminent. I said, "Antoinette, my love, what is life *for?* Answer me that?"

She just cupped her shrinking breasts and laughed, rather thinly I thought. She called me her "enormous whale baby." But there was a hungry glint sharking the blue waters of her eye. I whispered heavily into her ear, "Banana nut bread, my darling." I let the syl-

84

lables roll off my tongue like buttered peas. "Chicken Supreme," I said. "Braised Rabbit à la Provence. Shrimp Mull. Creamed Cod Halifax. Marzipan. Fondant. Marshmallow Mint Bonbons." These were some of her favorites.

I wore her down. "My darling," I said. "I could eat raw and rotting squaw fish, I am so very hungry." But Antoinette wanted to remain faithful to the famous internist. She said, "You are forgetting your promise to doctor, Gabe." And I replied, in the tragic vein, "I do not care about doctor, Antoinette! I am going to die of misery! This is no way to live!" Eventually I won her over. We gave up on the diet and went back to real food. "We are going to be happy again, darling, I promise you," I said. And for a while it was true.

Now hear this: I am hungry all the time. You may not choose to believe that. You might find such a statement a trifle on the bizarre side. But it is true. I simply do not stay full. I convert food to energy and bulk very quickly. I might go through a platter of oysters on the half shell, a tureen of minestrone, a tub of Texas hash, a loaf of Irish soda bread, three or four slabs of black bottom pie, ten cups of thick coffee, and do it all again in a couple of hours, believe what you will.

We were cruising around a pretty little inland town checking out Mexican restaurants. We'd found a lovely little place. But Antoinette had the blues. She said, "God, I just don't know, Commodore." Sometimes she called me Commodore. I found it pleasurable.

Something was eating her. She'd been depressed lately. Chewing, her face would sour. She'd put down her fork. "What is it, my darling?" I'd ask. "What's wrong? The meat not done well enough? That sauce flat? Light? Too sweet? Too tart?" She would shake her head, run her tongue over her teeth, lift her large breasts off her stomach as if trying to ease her breathing. "Oh, I don't know, Gabe. It's just me, I think." But this was not a satisfactory explanation.

86   And now, in Guzman's Authentic Sonoran Cuisine, she was balking at the menu. I ordered for her, which was something I hesitated to do. Ordering, after all, is half the *fun.*

"*Matambre,* por favor," I said to the waiter.

"*Matambre,*" said Antoinette, "is *not* Sonoran."

I looked at the waiter, a blond boy with large pimples on his neck. "She's right, you know," I said.

He shrugged. "Get the chicken enchiladas," he said. "It's the best thing on the menu."

"We can get chicken enchiladas anywhere," I said. "No, we'll try the *matambre.*"

In fact, it was wonderful *matambre.* My appetite increased. I ordered the *tostadas estilo,* which were made with pig's feet and beans. Antoinette ate as much as I did, but without evident relish.

We drove down to our condominium on San Diego Bay. I like the view, the great naval fleet, the fine tuna seiners, the pleasure craft. Sitting on our balcony, ten floors above the waterfront, I said, "Come on, Antoinette. Out with it. What's wrong, darling?"

There was a platter of cold tongue slices garnished with pimento olives and sweet gherkins between us. The boy had brought them. Antoinette was playing nervously with her diamonds. I tossed a piece of tongue into the air and caught it in my teeth. A small aircraft carrier was easing into the bay. I picked up the glasses to observe it.

"A," she said, "I have no friends. And, B, life between meals is empty."

I put down the glasses and handed her a cool slice of meat. "We have each other," I suggested. In retrospect, I imagine my tone was peevish.

She took a thoughtful bite of the tongue, but would not meet my eyes. The sun was warm on our large bodies. We liked to sit, without our clothing, on our little terrace, watching the boats. The boy, Wing, was as discreet as only the Chinese can be.

That night, Antoinette woke up in a thrashing sweat. I turned on the lights. "Feel my heart," she said. I put my hand on her breast. Something wild was walloping around in there.

"Take it easy, darling," I said, ringing for the boy. "Try to relax. Was it a dream?"

I had Wing fix a plate of leftover cold cuts for us. It was 3:00 A.M. I opened a quart of Pilsner. I covered two slices of rye with a nice hot mustard and then laid in the meat.

I heard her gagging in the bathroom. She stayed in

87

there for quite a while. Then she came into the kitchen and sat at the table. Her eyes were red and she smelled sour. "Fix me one of those," she said, looking at me with those direct blue challenging eyes that first attracted me to her four years ago.

"With or without," I said, holding up a jar of *Weinkraut*.

"With," she said, defiantly.

I breathed a sigh of relief. Whatever had troubled her sleep had passed. Or so I believed.

88

That summer I reached a happy three hundred. I felt good. Antoinette was only one-ninety, but she was coming along fine. When she hits two hundred, I told myself, look out! Her stomach blows out in front, shoving her loaflike breasts up high and handsome, the nipples spreading wide like brown saucers, and a gossamer rump so soft and creamy it could melt your heart and bring water to your mouth.

"Come over here, you lovely dumpling!" I'd command, and the walls of the condo would shake. I'd imagine the floor joists sagging, the wall studs splintering, the sheetrock crumbling, the roof tiles slipping off and crashing into the streets below.

By fall I made three-twenty and Antoinette reached two-oh-nine, equalling her previous high. We were never happier. We cavorted like honeymooners and ate like young whales. Dig in! Dig in!

We'd go to one of those smorgasbord places just for fun, the ones that advertise, "All You Can Eat for Five

Dollars." We loved to watch the manager's face sag as we lined up for seconds and thirds and fourths, on and on.

"Fifteen trips, Antoinette," I'd say, a friendly challenge, and she would sweetly reply, "You are on, Commodore!" And we'd fill and empty our trays fifteen times, *heaped,* while the manager would whimper to his girls and shake his head. Once we cleaned out an establishment's entire supply of veal-stuffed zucchini, which was supposed to be the specialty of the house. The manager was a skinny twerp who kept snapping a towel at flies. He didn't bother us. **89**

Now hear this: Skinny people can't be trusted. A man who can get along on cottage cheese, pears on lettuce, or chicken salad, bears watching. A man who keeps a girl's waistline is probably *sly.* I wouldn't touch one of those female skeletons you see in the ads. Like bedding down with tinker toys. I'd crush her dainty innards, her bones would go like twigs. All of them, the thin ones who are thin by choice, are *nibblers.* We once elected a tribe of fancy nibblers to high office and look where it got us. They make me gag.

Steak and potatoes, hot rolls and butter, cheese sauce and broccoli, stuffed eggplant, black bean soup, honey-glazed ham, Bavarian cream, chocolate butter sponge cake, jelly rolls, doughnuts, cookies, ice cream! Eat, eat, enjoy! Make that table groan. What do you have a mouth with teeth in it for? Whistling and smiling?

We were in a nice restaurant up north. Antoinette

had been feeling a little moody again and I thought a change of scene would do her good. She was up to two-twenty, an all-time high, and she never looked better. I was holding steady at three-forty-nine. Everyone has an upper limit, unless there's a problem and your glands explode on you.

Steak and kidney pie was the specialty of the house. The servings were generous enough, but we ordered, as usual, seconds and then thirds. Now, the thing is, we were very serious about eating. We would tuck our napkins in and we would *eat*. No small talk. No stopping for cigarettes. If we spoke at all it was to get the salt, the pepper, butter, soy sauce, and so on. Later, over coffee, we might talk.

We would get down, close to the plate, and we would keep the silverware moving. Lift dip, lift dip, lift dip. The object is to get the food into the stomach.

So I did not hear him when he first said it because I was occupied in the manner described. Then, when he raised his voice, I said, "Are you addressing me, sir?" He said he was. I dried off my mouth with my napkin and looked at him. I do not like to be interrupted when at table.

"You disgusting goddamn pigs," he said.

He was tall and skinny and had a cowboy-thin face that jutted out with years of lean living. I did not like his looks.

"You people look like you got life rafts tied around your necks you're so goddamn sinful fat."

90

Antoinette was still eating but her fork had slowed considerably.

"You supposed to be some kind of fucken sailor?" said the cowboy, sneering at me now and looking back to his table for approval. I sat erect in my chair, removed my napkin from my lap, and gazed coolly at him. "You got nearly everybody in this restaurant ready to puke, the way you pig down that food, admiral," he said, leering.

"That will be quite enough," I said.

He laughed at me and did something obscene. He threw his cigarette on my plate. Then he went back to his table which greeted him heartily, as a returning hero.

"Now hear this, Antoinette," I said. "We will not stand for this impudence. We have our dignity." Antoinette was white as her napkin and her eyes were teary. She had put her fork down. Her lip was trembling. She touched the sides of her neck with her careful fingertips.

"Life rafts?" she said.

I pushed away from the table and stood up. The skinny cowboy saw me coming but he turned his back deliberately as if I was not someone he should be concerned about. No one takes the fat man seriously.

"I believe this is yours, sir," I said.

I had my plate with me, complete with his dirty cigarette sticking out of the mashed potatoes. He turned slowly and looked at me in an offhanded way. Even his mouth was skinny, the lips like blades.

91

"What's that, pig face?" he said. The two skinny women and the skinny man who were at his table laughed. They were eating breaded fingerlings of some kind and crackers.

I took the back of his head in my left hand and with my right hand I shoved that plate full of ruined food into his face. His mouth yawned open for air under a smothering gray slick of potatoes and gravy. He was quite surprised by my action. Fat men are not generally regarded as quick, strong, or willing to retaliate. This is a common error. At two hundred pounds I can barely lift a kitten. At three-forty-nine, I am strong as a bear and quick enough. And, I am more than willing to demand satisfaction from the likes of the skinny cowboy.

He jumped to his feet and began throwing punches at me. But he was wild, hitting only my shoulders and chest which met his fists like sofa cushions. I pushed him off balance and kept pushing him until he was against a wall. Then I leaned, belly first, and the air whistled out of him. Antoinette came over then and pinched his cheek so hard that a welt appeared. He tried to kick me but his legs were about as dangerous as pencils. Behind us, his table was laughing and singing *Anchors Aweigh*.

I took Antoinette on a clothes-buying expedition to cheer her up. That ugly incident had made her blues return stronger than ever. At night she would wake up, filled with gas and sour dreams, gagging.

"These dresses," she said, holding several of the new items up. "They are *circus* tents." We were in our bedroom. I was in bed watching the morning news. The navy, I was sad to discover, was in full retreat before the budget-cutting demands of several skinny congressmen. They were denying the return of the beautiful battlewagons, calling them "fat missile targets." I made up my mind then and there to send telegrams to our legislators, urging them to bring the great wide-beam navy back. Then a commercial came on, diverting my thoughts. Ham and eggs in a sunny kitchen, whole wheat toast stacked like shingles, prune danish, fritters, and the lovely girl was taking potato pancakes out of the pan and carrying them to her smiling husband. My mouth watered.

Antoinette threw her new dresses aside and stood before the mirror. "Elephant," she said. She made her reflection jiggle and blur by rising up on her toes and letting her weight come down hard on her heels. The room vibrated. Then she began to prance. But it wasn't for fun. She was mocking herself. "Look at me!" she shouted with false merriment. "The elephant is dancing! Come one come all!" I thought she looked good. Lovely, in fact. Her rain barrel thighs roared across my field of vision. Her meal-sack breasts swung. Her dimpled rump seemed to fill the room. I was, quite frankly, aroused. I caught her by the wrist. "Oh no you don't!" she said. But I pulled her anyway. She came down, off-balance, and the wood slats of the bed cracked. Bang, and the bed came down. The room

93

quaked, and I imagined plaster dust graining the air of the room below. "No, Commodore!" she said. "I told you *no!*"

But the Commodore cannot be denied. "Jumbo lover," I whispered hoarsely into her tangled hair. I pinned her and our tonnage moved the seismographs of Spain.

She poked at her breakfast. I didn't like to see that. "Come, come, cupcake," I said. "What's wrong now?"

94

She looked at me across the laden table, her keen blue eyes gone soft and waxy. She touched her neck, an unconscious habit which began in the restaurant where I had been forced to discipline the skinny cowboy. I folded a piece of ham in half and speared it. She stabbed a fritter but she did not lift it to her lips. I chewed slowly, waiting. My patience, I confess, was wearing thin. Finally she put down her fork. I put down mine.

"My darling," I began. "Everything is either inside or it is outside. Make no mistake. If it is inside, it is being eaten. If it is outside, then it is either eating or waiting to eat. That is all anyone can say about it. The rest is manure. Things on the outside sooner or later find themselves in the inside. For, you see, everything gets its chance at being on the outside *eating,* or in the inside getting *eaten.* My darling, everything in the wide world is food. Us included. It is so very simple. I don't understand your confusion. We are lucky eaters now, but someday that will change. Dig in, my darling. It is the skinny people of the world who are stuffed to their eyes with illusions."

"We're freaks," she said. She left the table and went into the bathroom, where she retched.

I followed her to the bathroom and stood outside the door. "Are you making yourself vomit deliberately, Antoinette?" I asked. She did not reply. "I cannot sanction that, my darling. I can never sanction that." Still she did not reply.

Now hear this: Like most large men I'm tolerant and easy to get along with. But there is a line. If you are a skinny man you may not understand what I am saying here. Suppose, then, that you are a skinny dancer and you have married a skinny woman who is also fond of dancing. Then she decides, without consulting you, that she's tired of dancing and would rather sit down and eat. Soon she blossoms out to a healthy size eighteen or twenty and will not roll back the carpet when "The Lawrence Welk Show" comes on. You soon begin to feel stupid foxtrotting around your rumpus room with a barstool in your arms while the little woman has her face parked in the Kelvinator. Where is the little girl I married, the girl with the twinkling feet? you ask yourself. I shall tell you where she is. She has shipped out. That size eighteen or twenty with the drumstick in her hand is someone else. You have begun to sense this yourself and have taken to calling her the USS *Tennessee* or some such appellation meant to discourage her. But she is not discouraged. She has, perhaps, found herself a new companion, fat as herself, and you find them

95

together laughing wonderfully between mouthfuls of guacamole dip and tortilla chips. You're beginning to feel left out, are you not? You are disgusted by her. You are angry. Bitterness taints every bite of food you take and you grow skinnier and thus even farther away from her than ever. She asks, so innocently, what's wrong with you lately and you can only stare at her as if she is the last person in the world who has the right to ask that question. But you don't say a word because you are afraid, at this point, of what might happen if you open your mouth and let loose what's really troubling you. You have been *betrayed*, skinny, but you cannot say a word because that kind of betrayal is not punishable by God's law or by court martial.

A betrayer needs an ally. Our condominium had a number of candidates. Skinny food-haters, dozens of them. Fifty-year-old business executives with the bodies of schoolboys. Suntanned grandmothers in handkerchief bikinis. You never see them with food in their mouths. They live on vitamin supplements and protein tablets. One of these food-haters, Bessie Carr, gave Antoinette a subversive menu guaranteed to burn away her fat in a matter of weeks.

Antoinette refused to sit down with me and discuss it. "My darling, such diets are dangerous," I said. She looked at me with that challenge in her eyes, but it wasn't the same. There was no promise of fun in this new defiance. I felt sick at heart.

"You are the one, Gabe, who is digging his grave," she said. "And you are digging it with your mouth."

It was the realization of my worst fears. It had happened to me before, with others. *Am I cursed?* I asked myself. A trichinosis of self-doubt undermined the shank and brisket of my soul.

"Come, my darling," I said one morning, hoping to retrieve something of our former happiness, "let us do a Roly-Poly." But she looked at me with icy disgust. We hadn't done a Roly-Poly since our honeymoon and the two or three months of high excitement that followed. Yes, it is the pinnacle of frivolity, but I was desperate. My life, once again, was listing severely and threatening to capsize.

97

"Don't be vulgar," she said.

We used to do it in the hot tub. It was a game. We'd get about seven hundred tins of liverwurst and Wing would open them on the electric opener. Then we would cover ourselves with the tasty paste. We would roll and slide in the drained tub, nibbling liverwurst from each other until it was gone. It was the appetizer to afternoons filled with a smorgasbord of delights. I can remember Antoinette rolling like a dolphin and murmuring, "Yummers." Once we tried deviled ham, but it did not hold well to the skin. Those were the days. We were hot pink whales in a soupy bay.

But now her fat was going like lard in a skillet.

I began to eat for both of us, as if I could maintain her bulk by doubling my intake. By the time she dropped to one-fifty, I had climbed to three-eighty. I had passed my upper limit and the difference made me nervous and gassy.

Bessie Carr used to be fat herself. She brought over an album of snapshots showing her progress from a size twenty-two to a size nine. They were at the kitchen table, poring over the pictures. I said, leaning over them, "Now hear this: *there* is a woman after my own heart." I pointed to a picture of Bessie lying in a child's wading pool. Arms and thighs, like great roasts, fell over the sides of the inadequate pool. Her breasts expanded in the buoyancy of water. They looked like fine wheels of white cheese. The pale hummock of her belly was a vast, North African kingdom. She turned the pages, however, until she found herself thin. There she was, in a bikini, daylight blaring between her thighs even though she was standing in a normal way. So much daylight, quite frankly, that you could have placed an entire chicken between her upper thighs and it would have fallen to her feet without touching her! It was horrible, enough to make a leper queasy. I sighed regretfully and they both looked at me with undisguised scorn, and then pity.

"Adipose Tissue and Its Spiritual Implications," said a brochure I happened to find on Antoinette's vanity. I thumbed through it. There was a good deal of nonsense about something called "The Great Need." It seemed that we are very hungry, but not for food.

I went into the living room to point out the foolishness of such claims to her. She was sitting on the floor, before a black man with thickly lidded eyes. The

98

black man was on the TV set, speaking in low tones. He was wearing a turban of some kind.

"Antoinette," I said. "May I have a word with you?"

"Shh," she said.

"Please, my darling, we must discuss this thing."

She turned to me then, annoyed. "I am listening to Sri Raj," she said, sharply.

"I would rather you listened to *me* for a moment," I said, somewhat offended.

"No," she said. "I'm learning about it."

"It?" I asked, glancing at the black man who seemed on the verge of nodding off to sleep.

"Life, Gabe," she said. "I'm learning how to flower. The spiritual garden within is starving, according to Sri Raj."

I dropped the brochure. It fluttered to the floor beside her. "I'm going to have lunch," I said. "I'd like you to join me, Antoinette." I snapped off the TV set.

This angered her. "Don't call me Antoinette any more!" she said. "My name is Debbie! I've always *hated* that name Antoinette!"

"Have you now," I said.

"Yes I have! It's a pig's name! Farmers give their eight-hundred-pound sows names like Antoinette and Veronica and . . . and . . . *Emmeline!*"

"Do they," I said.

She turned the TV back on and the black man rolled into the screen. "Be joyful, then, as the little birds," he said.

I lunched alone. Wing, sensitive as ever to crisis, had made a wonderful Viennese *linzertorte,* one thousand calories per serving!

"Wing, old son," I said, affectionately. "Pack up my uniforms. I am afraid it's time to ship out."

And ship out I did. I am not such a fool as one who will humiliate himself before the inevitable. I bought into another condominium up the bay toward the city. Of course, I missed her terribly. I always miss them terribly. And why wouldn't I? It is no great pleasure to take your meals alone, is it? And what of the great restaurant hunts? The round robin eating binges? The king-size bed with double strength frame? Such a bed needs a great and ample queen.

Faithful Wing drove me about the city, looking for the new companion. Wing's careful manner at the wheel tended to hold my eagerness in check. The way he held to the speed limits, the sober way he lifted the gear lever, the delicate gloved hand on the wheel—all these things served as an example to my hasty mind. Haste, in such a weighty enterprise, can serve no good purpose. Had I taken more time to observe Antoinette four years ago, I might have detected the worm of discontent that finally poisoned our pleasant arrangement.

"I think we should look for a younger one this time, Wing," I said. "One with a simpler, more reliable outlook."

Wing understood immediately and turned the car toward the beach areas where the cheap, fast-food

100

restaurants thrive. We cruised the neon boulevards, scanning.

"Starboard bow, Wing," I said, pointing to a place called *Holy Cow!* It was a hamburger house shaped like Borden's Elsie. Sitting alone on the patio, a tray of giant cheeseburgers before her, was a likely prospect, a hefty redhead of eighteen or so. Her complexion was unfortunate, perhaps, but a year of clean, expensive food properly prepared would clear it up just fine. There were other young people there, but they sat tables away, avoiding her as though she had a dreaded 101 disease.

We sat in the parking lot for half an hour, simply observing her. Wing had the movie camera going and I was making copious notes. Even though I was wearing my elegant "King Edward" naval uniform, and would have made a stunning impression on her, we needed to exercise some empirical caution this time. But all the signs looked very good.

The longer I watched her lift those cheeseburgers to her lonely but shameless jaws, the more convinced I was that we were meant for each other. Her name was probably Kathy, Wendy, Jean, or Pam—something that did not give credit to her true nature. I thought about it for a while, then snapped my fingers, making Wing jump.

"Roxanne," I said. "We shall call her Roxanne."

Blind Euchre

NINA WEEMS WAKES, thinking *spider*. The boy hangs over her, descending, the small muscles of his face rigid. In the sun, next to the pool, lying on the dry, prickly grass, she has been having a dream about appliances: the smooth porcelained surfaces, the mute whir of motors, the precise ratcheting of cycling mechanisms, the sense of hidden mechanical intelligences that schedule unerring processes, the intimacy of the alternating current's hum. She has just touched a beautifully knurled handle that opens a vacuum-sealed door, when she wakes.

She shades her eyes against the sky. The boy is looking at her. *Spider,* she thinks, her heart believing it. The descent of the boy is windblown and slow. He hangs on visible thread, the trajectory of his fall slow yet steep, wind-guided, predatory. She reaches for her robe, succeeds only in opening herself to closer inspection, but he has already passed overhead and is now banking along the row of young eucalyptus that borders her property. His legs are padded, he wears jump boots, he is helmeted and gloved. A harness holds him to bright, triangular wings. The wings are made of white fabric ribbed with aluminum struts. When he passes over her again, he grins and attempts a gesture, but only his elbows move. His hands are tightly committed to the handgrips that guide his flight. His smile works against the frozen concentration of the rest of his face. Nina has not covered herself in time at all, and when her momentary fear passes, she throws the robe aside and curses, but not loudly, because, like the white ma-

106 chines, he is gone.

The game of Blind Euchre is particularly suited to hot weather, as it requires no skill and little thought. The cards are held so that each player sees every hand except his own. If he wins, it is always and entirely blind luck.

Nina put the game book back on the shelf and returned to the party. The men were becoming political and therefore nasty. Walt, her husband, looked bored. She knew he wasn't. Finally he moved. "Look," he said, "we need highly placed men who take corruption for granted. If you want to survive, this is where you start. This is square one." A drunk physician, spilling his drink, said, "You arrogant bastard, Weems."

The women moved to the kitchen. Lana Sternlech made the coffee. The conversation, which had been about girlhood wishes coming true, changed abruptly when Nina entered. "This incredible *house!*" someone said, feigning jealous admiration. "Nina, you absolute duchess!" Someone else said, "Six hundred seventy eight thou." Nina took the cards out of the odds-and-ends drawer, cut to the five of clubs, put them back. "Look at the brutal *ring!*" said a woman Nina had never seen before. The woman, tall with steel-gray hair pulled tightly back, held Nina's hand up. The ring *had* once belonged to the duchess of Romagna. It was a large, crested, black stone. There was a hidden stem that opened a secret compartment. When the conversation shifted to hot weather recipes, Nina turned her back to the others, pressed the hidden stem, and poured a fine white powder into her drink.

She went to the double glass doors, slid them apart, and stepped into the arboretum. There was no wind but something moved in the branches of the fruitless mulberry. Nina circled the tree. There was a dark shape fastened to the narrow trunk, about halfway up and obscured by the leaves and branches. The moon flared behind the row of eucalyptus. The air was sweet with night-blooming jasmine. The dark shape in the mulberry tree spoke to her.

"What would this place be called, love?" it asked.

"Ciudad de Sobrante," she said.

"And what does that mean in the vernacular, darling?"

"It means 'City of Excess.' But the developer does not encourage literal translation."

"The same word in two languages often produces what we might call independent responses, is that what the developer claims?"

"My husband is the developer," Nina said. "Who are you?"

"Who *would* I be, tied to a tree, my child?"

Nina walked to the pool. The figure in the tree came down, breaking small branches in his descent. He was a short, stocky man wearing horn-rimmed glasses. He followed Nina to the edge of the pool. He slipped his arm around her waist and tried to kiss her on the neck. She leaned away from him. He took her glass and drank from it. The knuckle of his thumb nudged her breast.

"I've had a checkered career, love," he said, morosely. "My name is Mel Cantini. I once was a semi-narian, S.J., but switched to physics. I taught small-particle theology at Berkeley. But I lost the faith *again*. Now I sell real estate. Big time. I work for your husband, darling. I am his ace, so to speak."

Mel Cantini took off his clothes. He climbed up on the diving platform and made a speech about how God made the profit motive possible by creating vast tracts of linked atoms. Then he dove. He struck the water at a comic angle and sank to the bottom of the pool where he sat, playing an imaginary violin. He still had his glasses on.

Nina went to the garage. She climbed into the Alfa and backed out into the street. Its throaty roar suited her mood. For the rest of the evening she drove the streets of the development, shifting the gears smartly, taking corners at near dangerous speeds. She felt that she was a very good driver. She sang the names of the brand new streets. Timar. Pinzon. Reyezuelo. Corneja. Halcón. Grulla.

A hill studded with boulders forms the north wall of Ciudad de Sobrante. An eight-foot wall of white adobe seals off the rest of the development from the dry rolling hills of mesquite, sage, yarrow, amaranth, and nopal. Seventeen miles of two-lane highway connects the development to La Corteza, the nearest town. The highway has twenty-eight curves, four grades that require at least one downshift, a crossroad that leads in one direction to the sea, in the other to the desert. Motion and sound are rarities here. Once a day, a passenger jet makes its small thunder overhead. Nina does not like this jet. She feels that it intrudes upon the massive inland silences she has come to love. Five minutes before the jet is due, she puts Mozart on the stereo, volume up. When the tone arm lifts and is returned to its resting position, the silence floods the sky again, roars into the house, and she moves in it, like a swimmer. Then she goes out into the kitchen and fixes herself a sandwich and begins to think about dinner. Walt is easy to please. Salisbury steak is his favorite, along with steamed vegetables, and a nice salad. He was not born with money. His success in real estate has come in recent years. Walt is tall, athletic, handsome, fifty. He was an all-conference end and had played in the Rose Bowl. He flies his own plane, a Cessna, to Los Angeles, San Diego, Palm Springs, and Las Vegas. He knows Gene Autry personally. Walt and Nina have been married nine years. Nina is thirty-eight. "I am a lucky woman," she tells herself, knowing that it is absolutely true.

109

Here's one for history buffs: Look through your old
magazines and newspapers and cut out all the
pictures of the famous men and women of the last
century you can find—everyone from Decatur to Li
Hung Chang, from Daniel Boone to Kruger, from
Queen Hortense to Helen Gould, from Coxey to
Kipling. Clip the names off and make frames for
them of pasteboard and gilt paper. Write invitations
on the backs of these cards. To wit: You are invited
to attend the opening of the Nineteenth Century
110 *Portrait Gallery. R.S.V.P. (required). Then clear*
your drawing room (you have one, yes?) of all its
furniture and pictures. We shall strive for austerity.
Make a pedestal and stand a little girl on it dressed
as the Goddess of Fame. Drape the girl in white,
knot her hair in the Grecian style. She will
interrogate the guests as they enter. If they do not
know "who" they are, certain punishments will be
exacted.

"There is a man here to see Mr. Weems," said Gan-
dolph, the guard. "He says he represents a firm called
Electro-Tell." Nina had the guard spell Electro-Tell.
"What does it mean?" she asked.
"Something to do with domestic security, he says,"
said Gandolph.
"My husband is in Phoenix," she said.
She heard the guard tell this to the man. The guard
sounded arrogant and threatening. "Mrs. Weems, he

says he wants to talk to you, if that's okay. Should I get rid of him?"

"No," she said. "Send him up."

"Maybe you'd better take a peek at him, Mrs. Weems," said the guard in a hushed voice.

Nina turned on the TV set and switched to channel D. The view from the gate showed a white sedan. Sitting behind the wheel was a large black man with a shaved head. He wore sunglasses and chin whiskers.

Nina laughed. "You're hopeless, Gandolph. Send the gentleman up."

Five minutes later her doorbell rang. She answered it. A tall, glistening man stood before her holding a large briefcase.

"So, you're the menacing Negro," she said, smiling.

"Correct," said the man, returning her smile.

"Gandolph worries a lot," Nina explained, somewhat apologetically.

"Gandolph is the tiny Prussian at the gate?"

"Correct," said Nina. "But that's what we pay him for, isn't it?"

"Absolutely, madam," said the tall, courteous man, bowing.

Nina opened the door wider and let him in.

"My name is Joseph," he said. "Field representative for Electro-Tell, Incorporated. Palo Alto—Silicon Valley to most. We are into home security systems."

He sat down on the sofa and snapped open his case. He spread his long narrow hands over it, palms down,

111

and said, "Voilà, Mrs. Weems. A box full of magic."

Nina admired his incredibly long fingers. She thought of the genie in *Arabian Nights.*

He lifted a wallet-sized device from the case. "First, let us look at the Portable Ear. It provides a wide spectrum of information for your security needs, relative to the intruder, once he has gained access." He opened the device and touched a red switch. A light began to strobe. "You sleep with this under your pillow, my dear, and it whispers a lullaby of alarms." He returned it to the case. "Secondly," he said, "we have the Compression Analyzer. Any sound, within or beyond the range of human hearing, is instantly analyzed for content and purpose." He held up a narrow panel with small meters on it. "And these," he said, "are the magic beans." He held up two small oval-shaped buttons. "You put these into your ears. They are Remote Adapters. You can stroll in your garden and be one hundred percent *aware.*"

He removed a larger mechanism from his case. It had moveable parts. A device telescoped out of one of the parts. An egg-shaped housing was mounted on a tripod. He pressed a toggle and the egg-shaped housing began to rotate. A high electrical whine filled the room. On one of the components there were dials that gave readings in terms of azimuth, range, elevation, and decibels. "Remote Intention Discriminator," he said. "RID, for short."

Nina said, "I don't understand any of this."

The man laughed pleasantly. "A laser penetration device," he said. "The probe will automatically seek a resonator. The window, for example, of your neighbor's house. Sound produced within the house will modulate, through the resonating medium, the beam's frequency. This modulation is translated into intelligible information by the receiver."

"It's a *bug*," said Nina.

The man frowned. "Crude term, ma'am. But here, let me demonstrate."

Something electrified the back of her neck, making gooseflesh rise. "Please do, Joseph," she said, pushing herself deeper into the cushions of the couch.

He smiled as though he were looking directly at her, but he wasn't. He made some adjustments to the apparatus, then handed Nina a set of headphones. She put them on. He went to the window and opened the drapes. He set the tripod with its rotating egg next to the window. The egg stopped turning.

In the earphones, Nina heard the voice of Lana Sternlech. She was speaking to her dog, Rajah. "I'm asking you to show me your tongue, Rajah," Lana said.

"Her dog is sick again," Nina said.

"Please, show mother your *tongue*, Rajah!" said Lana Sternlech, anguished.

"An ancient poodle," Nina explained, and Joseph shrugged sympathetically.

"If you do not show me your tongue, mother will restrict your toys!"

Nina removed the earphones. "This is evil," she said.

Joseph shrugged. "We live in a fallen world, ma'am," he said.

"And so we might as well make the most of it, right?"

Joseph smiled. "In such a world, one must be wary."

"I want it," Nina said. "I'll give you a check."

In their nine years of marriage, Nina had never seen Walt angry, really angry. They had driven over to La Corteza for a late afternoon drink. They had taken the Alfa, Nina behind the wheel. She cut one minute eighteen seconds off her best time. They celebrated with a round of margaritas. Someone in the bar set off a string of firecrackers close to the Weems's table. Walt turned white, his knuckles whitening on his glass, the bridge of his nose white. The man started to light more firecrackers. It was the third of July. There had been a small parade which would be repeated tomorrow. The tavern was crowded with Americans. A red-faced man in mechanic's overalls and an Uncle Sam hat joined them at the table. He was drunk and he touched Nina's shoulder several times, squeezing it suggestively. Once he whispered into her ear, "I've seen you before, haven't I? I'm a mechanic. You've got something I can fix, don't you?"

More firecrackers went off. Walt stood up, trembling with anger. He found the man with the firecrackers and took away his matches. The man slapped Walt on the side of the neck, weakly. Walt spun the man around in a complete circle, then knocked him down. A tiny blonde woman grabbed Walt by the shirt and said, "Cocksucker!" Walt shoved her down on top of the fallen man. Someone threw a glass full of tequila into his face. The woman on the floor, her skirt up on her hips, yelled murderously, "Cocksucker! Cocksucker!" A mariachi band blared out something that sounded like the American national anthem. Several sailors stood up and saluted. Nina pulled Walt out of the bar. When they reached the Alfa, they found a baby wrapped in newspapers lying on the front seat. It was a 115 Mexican baby, no more than a few weeks old. It was crying. Walt picked the baby out of the seat and handed it to the first woman he saw. He gave the woman a dollar. The woman held the baby awkwardly. She was about sixty years old. Walt and Nina got into the car. The woman shrugged and put the baby down on the sidewalk.

Walt floored the Alfa and popped the clutch. They jerked away from the curb. Walt was growling between his teeth. "Give me the goddamn Hilton next time," he said. "I've had it with these dumps."

Let's have a Donnybrook! Throw open your home to all the neighbors! Ask them to wear the green. Arrange a number of stalls and booths, and have these presided over by "market women." They shall wear shawls and their feet shall be bare. Have the gray-haired ladies sitting about knitting and trading gossip. A noisy peddler banging his pots and pans.

*Arrange live stock pens with a live pig, geese, and
chickens. Have a "goose girl" in charge. (This
perhaps is the hostess.) Serve Irish stew, boiled
potatoes, fish, cakes, and of course, a good Catholic
whiskey. Arrange the Blarney Stone in the midst of a
bog, the more pitfalls the better. Set two of the stouter
men to sparring and bragging. And now who comes
in but the Lord Mayor himself! Faith! The jigg's up,
boy-o! Now we dance.*

116   There is a movie on about Lord Baltimore or somebody starring Tyrone Power or somebody. A sandstorm
is trying to come over the mountains from the desert.
The temperature is one hundred and ten. The wind
whistles in the eaves, archways, and casements. Nina
turns up the volume with the remote control. The
announcer says, "Maryland is such a pretty name for a
state, isn't it folks?" Nina agrees. "But give me the dry
desert heat and empty miles," she says, shutting off the
sound as the commercial comes on.

A wind chime falls into a cactus. Nina goes into the
kitchen to heat the coffee. Walt has been gone for days,
talking to important people in the north. Something
scrapes against the house. There is a clubbing noise and
then a child's voice screeching curses above the wind.

The trees of the arboretum are blowing first one way
and then the other with the fierce wind. Beyond the
trees, near the pool, there is a boy on his hands and
knees, crawling desperately but making no progress.
He is tangled in his wings. The wings rise and fall, rise
and fall, as the twisting wind harrasses them.

Nina goes out to help him. "I hit your antenna," the boy says, an accusation. His nose is bleeding and his arms are scraped. Nina brings the boy into the cool house and makes him some cocoa. He is fifteen or sixteen, but small and delicate. He has sensitive but hostile eyes. He drinks his cocoa silently at the kitchen table, looking, from time to time, out the sliding glass doors at his damaged wings crabbing along in the grass.

"Daedalus," Nina says. "I ought to be very annoyed with you."

"June," says the boy, sheepishly. "My name is June de la Mer." 117

"My God," says Nina, touching his sandy hair.

"What?"

"That's beautiful. June de la Mer."

The boy winces, lifts his large cup to his lips. His pale, intense eyes, however, do not leave her face.

"You shouldn't use your wings in such dangerous wind, June," Nina scolds.

The boy feels complimented. He tells her about his wings, revealing a technical sophistication and a dedication to hang-gliding that she finds moving. He speaks of camber, lift, interface stress, glide angle, metal fatigue, and thermals. He speaks rapidly and without hesitation.

Nina sees the unformed man lurking in the boy. A pilot, a naval officer, a boss, a technical advisor to corporations. The self-confident intelligence is there already, like a stainless steel armature. Nina considers taking the boy to her bed, a gift to Daedalus.

"What do you like best in school?" she asks.

He tells her that history is his favorite subject. He finds that science classes are worthless because they are geared for those of marginal ability. He speaks of Portugal.

"Portugal," he says, his immature voice rapturous, "is not typical of the Latinic countries. It seems almost cut off from normal time and space. They went their own way. I see it as our Tibet. It isn't so much a nation as it is a principle of order." His light gray eyes are on her, judging her response. He pushes his empty cup toward her. "When the Portuguese want something, they usually get it."

Nina is stirred by his little speech. Not by the ideas, but by the singular force behind it.

"Daedalus," she says. "Would you teach me how to fly?"

The boy looks out at his rippling wings. "Sure," he says. "It's easy."

Walt sits up suddenly. Nina turns on the night table lamp. "Christ," he says, touching his chest.

He rolls out of bed onto the floor. "Oh, Jesus," he says, grimacing.

"What is it?" Nina says.

"I don't know, I don't know."

"Your heart? Walt?"

"It's my heart. Oh, Christ, it's my heart."

"I'll call Jerry."

"No! Don't call that prick. He'd love to come here and gloat. I won't have that prick gloating."

"I'll call another doctor."

"Don't call anybody. They all gloat. They love it, they love to see the big ones go down. Jesus."

Walt, sitting on the floor, is breathing easier now. He stands up slowly. "Maybe it was my gall bladder. I've been eating pure grease for a week."

"Does it still hurt?"

"Feels like a hot poker." He puts on his robe and goes out to the game room. Nina follows. Walt lies down on a couch, picks up the remote control for the TV. "Get the Chevalier tape, would you honey?" he says.

119

Nina gets the Maurice Chevalier tape and plugs it into the video cassette recorder. An old man appears on the screen. He is dancing laboriously around a small stage. He sings, "tout va bien pour vous, tout va bien pour moi," and Walt smiles.

"I love that old fart," Walt says, relaxing now as the hot pain subsides. In a faltering, dreamy baritone, Walt sings, "Thank heaven, for little girls."

Walt wants to show Mel Cantini how to box. Mel backs away, toward the bar. "No way, boss," he says. But Walt insists, makes Mel hold his hands up. He shows Mel the proper stance. He jabs at Mel's face and Mel flinches. Walt's loose fingers graze Mel's face, again and again, and Mel blinks. "You win, boss," he says, laughing, but Walt moves in with short uppercuts and hooks and right crosses, all of which fall inches short of the target. Mel turns his back, his face grim. He walks to the bar and pours himself a large gin and tonic. Walt trails him, showing classy footwork. Nina steps in front of him. "You're being a pest," she says.

"This is my wife, everybody!" Walt shouts to the crowd, a wide, vicious smile on his face.

Later, Walt tells several young men, earnestly, "If you're not first, then you're tied for last. That's *the* rule of this business. Your ulcers, gentlemen, are your battle ribbons. There is no such thing as second place. There is first, and there is last."

120   They were several thousand feet over the coast of southern California. It was Elmo Ripley's plane, one of Walt's partners. Elmo had not sobered up from the previous night in Vegas. They were all headed for Santa Cruz, for a "work party," as Walt put it. "Fun and business mix, contrary to the old saw," he said.

Elmo wanted to arm wrestle. He and Walt went into the passenger compartment. "Who's going to fly the plane?" asked Peggy Ripley, Elmo's wife.

"Let Nina fly it. She knows how to fly, I understand," said Walt.

Nina found herself alone at the controls. She had been sitting next to Elmo in the copilot's seat when he got up and went back to find Walt. Peggy Ripley came up and sat down next to her. "Do you really know how to fly?" she said.

"No," said Nina, angry.

"Nothing to it, doll," said Peggy. "You just keep the nose on the horizon and that needle above your right knee on zero."

"I think the next omni station is Santa Barbara," Elmo called from the back of the plane.

Nina gripped the wheel. The engines began to labor.

"You've let the horizon get away from you, doll," said Peggy Ripley.

Nina pushed the wheel forward. The engines began to rise in pitch. It was a frightening sound. The horizon rose to the top of the windshield, like water filling a glass tank.

"You're diving, doll," said Peggy.

121

Hold this party in the attic, if you have one. The invitations should be in the form of warrants. When the guests arrive, tell them they will be expected to pay for everything. Ha ha. Start them off on a fox hunt or a goose chase. Take out your prepared narrative. This is how things will be carried out—no excuses. Take out the list of animals. Whisper to each guest his animal identity; e.g., "You, Ericka, are a wombat." Tell each guest that when the animal he's picked is called, that he must imitate the animal in some unusual but characteristic way. What we mean here is that a seal barking for bonbons will not be tolerated. Be clever. Show a display of sexual aggression or how a bullock screams before the butcher's ax. The best "animal" will be made Emperor King.

When did this begin? Why? Will it go on? Nina, lying under Mel Cantini in a La Corteza hotel room does not see clearly how this happened. And so suddenly. Who suggested it? Why did it seem like a good idea? Will there be consequences?

Mel is overweight and is laboring. His thrusts are irregular, suggesting fatigue. Then, suddenly, he stops. He rolls off, breathing heavily.

"Did I hear you say something?" he asks. "Did you say something like, 'what for?' Did I hear that?"

Nina rises and goes into the tiny bathroom.

"Are you getting even with him, maybe?" he says to the closed door. "Is that it?" He lights a cigarette. "Maybe we're both getting even. But I doubt it."

Nina comes out of the bathroom. "No, that's not it," she says. "I like you, in a way. That's enough, isn't it?"

"Hell, we all like each other in a way," Mel says, a bit downcast. "That's not a factor. I think Walt is a peachy fellow, really. He's going to make me rich."

"He's a winner," says Nina. Then she smiles. "But you don't believe there are any winners, do you?"

"There's the rich and the poor. There's the happy and the sad. There's the strong and the feeble. The fucked and the unfucked. And so on. This can't be denied."

"But winners?"

Mel stubs out his cigarette. "Nothing is necessary, anything is possible, and no one is accountable."

"You don't fool anyone, Mr. Cantini," Nina says, laughing.

"No, I mean it. It's my credo, my rule book."

"Why real estate, then?"

"I like outdoor work."

They dress and go down to the bar for a round of margaritas. The tequila heats them again and they go back to their room.

"Maybe it's Mexico," Nina says.

"Ah," Mel says, stringing kisses down her spine. "The fatalistic air. You breathe it. It goes down into your marrow. All that *Norte Americano* blather, gone. Only the eternals are taken seriously here."

"Like love?"

"Like love."

123

"These little parties are getting wilder and wilder," a hysterical woman said.

An ape and a bear carried Nina into the game room. They dropped her on the pool table and would not let her sit up. The ape shoved the bear. "You asshole," said the ape. "Let me handle this." The bear dragged the ape away. They rolled on the floor, laughing in their animal heads. Walt, dressed as a giant lobster, came in, a bottle of gin in one of his pincers. "I'm going to break somebody's back," he said.

Nina dozed. She had emptied the contents of her ring into her last drink. Her lips felt numb. She felt slightly paralyzed. She was alone in the game room. Then she was not alone. Someone was standing directly behind her whistling a melody from some Wagner piece. She dozed again. She dreamed about white appliances. Her right hand was tight on a beautifully knurled handle. The door it was attached to was coming open. She realized, suddenly, that she wanted very much to wake up. But she was unable to wake herself. Her arms and legs would not move. Her lips would not move. Her heart was speeding up, but there was nothing she could do about it, not even scream.

The lights of the Ciudad are below her. The party has moved to the hillside, among the granite boulders. The men are carrying lanterns and torches made of newspapers. The women are singing. Mel Cantini is wearing a monk's habit and sandals. "These parties are getting wilder and wilder," says a woman. A great, triangular shape is silhouetted against the light from the torches and lanterns.

"Strap it here," someone says, and Nina feels the coarse canvas belts pressing her breasts flat.

Several strong men are holding her aloft. She hears Mel Cantini say, "The departed left no forwarding address."

"These parties are getting wilder and wilder," says a laughing woman.

A young man kneels between Nina's legs, hefting a stone. "It's a lovely thirty-pound stone!" he announces. "Kiss it, mama."

"Get out of there, you idiot," says Mel Cantini. "Break his spine for that, Walt."

"I will when he grows one," says Walt, scornfully.

Mel puts a drink to her lips. "This will brace you for it, darling," he says.

"Enough of that," says Walt. "It's time for the grand finale." His eyes twinkle red in the torchlight.

124

A man with strong hands and arms is drawing the laces together at her spine. The canvas belts crush the air out of her lungs. Six men, holding her aloft by her thighs and arms, begin to trot through the field of stones. They urge her to fly.

"She's *good*," someone says. "God, she's really *good!*"

"Practice, practice, practice," says Walt.

Nina feels the night air fill the nylon wings as the cords at her spine jerk her away from the hill. A heavy cheer bursts from the darkness below.

A thermal wind gives her unexpected altitude, and the voices from below fade. Ahead of her, the moonlit hills are the color of talc.

She sails toward them. She guides herself bravely into her own dream, discovering it, knowing that there will be no way, no way at all, to get back.

Billy Ducks
Among the Pharaohs

THE BILLETDOUX FRONT YARD should have told me right away that the job wouldn't amount to much. The lawn was overgrown with spikey weeds, what grass there was had died a number of seasons ago, deep tire ruts oozy with muck grooved the yard, and a rusty tub filled with crankcase oil sat on the warped porch. But I had just turned eighteen and was still untuned to the distress signals the world volunteers with unfailing reliability.

Price Billetdoux—he pronounced his name "Billy Ducks"—answered my knock. He was in pajamas and bathrobe, even though it was midafternoon. He stood before me, dark and grizzled, blinded by ordinary daylight. When he focused on me, he shoved his hand into his robe pocket as if looking for a gun.

"I'm the one who called," I explained quickly. I held up the newspaper and pointed to his ad. "I want to try it, photography."

"Amigo," he said, pulling a crumpled pack of Camels from his bathrobe, "come in."

I followed him into the kitchen. There was a plump girl at the stove peeling an egg off a skillet. She was also in pajamas and robe. She had stringy, mud-colored hair and very small feet. She looked about twelve. I figured she was Billetdoux's daughter.

"Pour us a couple of cups of java, will you Shyanne?" he said to her.

The girl dragged two cups out of the sink, rinsed them, and filled them with inky coffee. She moved listlessly, as if she had been sick and was just recovering.

130   Billetdoux lit his Camel, drank some coffee, made a face. He had haggard, bloodshot eyes. Dark, tender-looking pouches hung like pulpy half-moons under them. He squinted at me through the smoke, sizing me up. Then he explained the job. No salary. No insurance. No fringe benefits. No vacations. Everything I made would be a percentage of the gross. I would go from door to door, trying to get housewives to let me take pictures of them and their children. I would offer them an eight-by-ten glossy for only one dollar. That was the "bait." How could they refuse? But when I went back with the print, I would also have a portfolio of five-by-sevens, three-by-fives, plus a packet of wallet-size prints. The portfolio would cost anywhere from $5.95 to $11.95, depending on how many prints were purchased. Of course, if they accepted only the eight-by-ten "bait" item for a buck, there was no profit or commission.

"You can make a hundred or more a week if you're good," Billetdoux said. "And your hours are your own.

I've got a boy over in Sulphur Springs who nets one-fifty."

I admitted that I didn't know the first thing about taking pictures, but he fanned the air between us as if to not only clear the cigarette smoke but also the heavy cobwebs of confusion from my mind. "I can show you how to take pictures of a prize-winning quality in ten minutes, amigo. The job, however, is salesmanship, not art."

He took me down to the basement where he kept his "photolab." We had to pass through a hall that led to the back of the house. Halfway down the hall he stopped next to a door and tapped on it softly. Then he pushed it open an inch. I saw a woman with wild gray hair lying in bed. She was propped up on several pillows. She also had the sickroom look, just as the girl did. Her eyes were dark and lusterless and her skin looked like damp paper. There was a guitar lying across her lap.

131

"I've got to break in a new boy, Lona," Billetdoux said. "I'll get you some breakfast in a little bit." Lona, who I assumed was Billetdoux's wife, let her head loll off the pillows until she was facing us. She didn't speak, but her large, drugged-looking eyes seemed to be nursing specific, long-term resentments. After Billetdoux closed the door, he whispered, "Lona is very creative, amigo."

The basement was a hodge-podge of equipment, stacked boxes, file cabinets, work tables, half-finished carpentry projects, all of it permeated with the smell of chemicals. He shoved stacks of paper around on his desk until he found a small brass key. He opened a cabinet with this key and took out a camera. "We'll start you on the Argus," he said. "It's simple to use and takes a decent picture. Later on, if you stick with me, I'll check you out on a Rolleiflex."

He took me step by step through the Argus, from film loading to f-stop and shutter speed. "I'll go around with you the first few days," he said, "to show you the ropes. Then you're on your own. You're a nice-looking boy— the housewives will trust you." He winked, as if to suggest that trusting the likes of me and Billetdoux would be the biggest blunder a housewife could make.

We went back upstairs to the kitchen. "How about some breakfast?" he said.

I looked at my watch. "It's after three," I said.

"It is? No wonder I'm so hungry. Where the hell does the time run off to, amigo? Well, how about some lunch then? Could you go for a bite of lunch?"

"Sure," I said. I hadn't eaten breakfast either.

"Shyanne," he called. "Honey, would you come in here?"

She came in, looking slightly more haggard than when I first saw her.

"Shy, hon, fix us some lunch, will you? The boy here and I are starved."

"There's no bread," she said. "Or meat."

Billetdoux pulled open a cupboard door. "How about some Cheerios, then?" he said.

"Fine by me," I said.

He poured out three bowls of the cereal, then added milk. He handed one bowl to Shyanne. "Here, hon," he said. "Take this in to Lona, will you? She hasn't eaten since yesterday."

"No one's eaten since yesterday," she said. "Except me, if you want to count that measly egg."

Billetdoux grinned darkly at me, embarrassed. "Time to make a grocery run, I guess," he said.

We ate in silence. The milk on my cereal was slightly sour. A big, late summer fly droned past my ear and landed upside down on the table where it exercised its thick, feeble legs. A loud, nasty voice broke into the homely sound of our spoons tapping on the Melmac bowls. I heard the word "swill" hiss from the hallway. Shyanne came in, carrying the bowl of Cheerios. "Lona doesn't want cereal," she said, dumping the milk-bloated O's into the sink. "She wants Spam and eggs."

"What about toast?" Billetdoux said.

"Right. Toast, too, and hashbrowns."

He leaned forward, his eyes damp and tired looking. "Listen, kid," he said. "Can you loan me ten bucks until tomorrow? I'm a little short. I had to get a new transmission put in my car last week. Cost? It's legal robbery."

I took out my wallet. I still had about fifty dollars from my last job. I gave him ten.

"Thanks, amigo. Splendid. I won't forget this. This is above and beyond, amigo."

Shyanne plucked the ten out of his hand. "I'll go to the store," she said.

133

"Don't forget cigarettes," Billetdoux said.

Billetdoux told me how to snowjob a housewife, but the first door we knocked at was answered by a kid of about six or seven. I looked at Billetdoux, who was standing right behind me. "What do I do now?" I asked.

"Is your old lady at home, buster?" Billetdoux said.

The kid started to close the door. His little sister, naked and grimy, stood behind him, a gray pork chop in her muddy hand. Pale green bulbs of snot plugged her nostrils.

Billetdoux pulled a bent Tootsie Roll out of his pocket and gave it to the boy. The boy accepted it, visibly relaxing his doorway vigil. "Mummy not home, huh?" Billetdoux said. "Well, that's all right. That's no problem at all." To me he whispered, "In a way, amigo, it makes our job easier."

He pushed the door all the way open and we went in. "Set the flood lamps up like I told you," he said. "Remember, the mainlight sits back about seven feet. Put the fill-light about three feet behind it, but over to the right. That way we get an arty shadow."

I opened the equipment case I'd carried in and took out the lamps. I set them up on their stands. While I was doing this, Billetdoux set two chairs up in the middle of the living room. I moved the two lamps so that they were the proper distance from the chairs.

"Hey, buster," Billetdoux said to the boy. "Your sis got any clothes? Why don't you be a good scout and

134

hunt up some drawers for her, okay? We don't want to take what you might call filthy pornographic pictures, do we? And wash off her snot-locker while you're at it."

I set up the tripod and attached the Argus to it. The boy pulled a pair of pink panties on his sister. I took the pork chop out of her hand and set it on the coffee table. I used my own handkerchief to clean her nose. Billet-doux sat them down in the chairs. He stepped back and looked at them in the unmerciful blare of the flood lamps. "Good enough," he said. "Now, amigo, you are going to have to work on their expressions. Right now they look like starving Lithuanian refugees about to be processed into dog food by the SS. Not a cheery sight, is it?"

"Smile, kids," I said, bending to the Argus.

The kids looked dead in the viewfinder.

"*Smile* won't get it, amigo," Billetdoux said. "Smile is the kiss of death in this racket. You might as well ask them to whistle Puccini. No, you've got to bring out some personality, whether they've got any or not. You want to get something on their faces their mama will blink her eyes at in wonder. You want her to think that she's never really *seen* her own kids. Got the idea?" He knelt down in front of the kids and raised his hands up like an orchestra leader. "I want you kids to say something for Uncle Billy Ducks, will you?" The kids nodded. "I want you kids to say, 'Hanna ate the whole banana,' and I want you to say it together until Uncle Billy Ducks tells you to quit, okay?"

135

He stood up and said to me, "Take ten shots. Press the shutter button between 'whole' and 'banana.' Got it? Okay kids, start saying it." He raised his hands like an orchestra leader again and started the kids chanting the phrase. I hit the button too soon the first time, too late the second, but I gradually fell into the rhythm of their sing-song chant and was able to snap their pictures on the simulated smile generated when their mouths were opened wide on "whole" but starting to close for "banana."

136 I took ten pictures, then shut off the floods. Billetdoux was nowhere in sight. I felt uneasy about our being alone in the house with these kids. The heat of the floods had raised a greasy sweat on my back. Then Billetdoux came in. He had a pork chop in his hand. "There's some grub in the icebox, amigo, if you're for it," he said. "Make yourself some lunch." He bit into the pork chop hungrily. "I'll say this," he said, chewing fast. "The lady of the house knows how to fry a chop."

Billetdoux began rummaging through the drawers of a built-in sideboard that filled one wall of the small living room. "Hello there," he said, lifting a pair of candle holders out of a drawer. "Take a look, amigo." He hefted the candle holders as if weighing them for value. "Solid sterling, I believe," he said. He slipped them into his jacket pocket. Then he continued rummaging. The kids didn't pay any attention to him. They were still mumbling "Hanna ate the whole banana," as they watched me taking down the floods. I worked fast, sweating not just from heat now but from fear. "Hello

hello hello," Billetdoux crooned, dumping the contents of a big black purse onto the dining room table. "Coin of the old realm—silver dollars, amigo. Cartwheels. 1887. The real McCoy. The landowners here appear to be silver hoarders . . . shameful, no?" He picked up one of the silver dollars and bit it lightly. Then he shoveled the big coins into a pile and began to fill his pockets with them. "It's rotten to hoard money like this when there's so much real need in the world today," he said, his voice husky with moral outrage.

"Let's go," I said.

"One momento, por favor, kid," he said. "Nature calls." He disappeared into the back of the house. I snapped the equipment case shut, picked it up and headed for the door. I heard the sound of water hitting water followed by a toilet flushing. As I opened the front door I believed I could hear him brushing his teeth vigorously.

I waited outside, down the street. He showed up in a few minutes, his pockets bulging, another pork chop in his felonious hand. He had an electric frying pan under one arm and a desk encyclopedia under the other. "You didn't get any lunch, amigo," he said, his forehead furrowing with concern. "What's the matter, no appetite? You got a flu bug? Here, this chop is for you. You need to keep up your strength in this business."

I put the equipment case down. "You're a thief!" I said, realizing that this surge of righteousness was about ten minutes late.

He lowered the pork chop slowly. He looked aston-

137

ished, then deeply hurt. "Say again, amigo? Billy Ducks a *thief?*"

"You heard me," I said, unmoved by his dismay.

"You're too harsh, amigo. I assure you it will all go toward an excellent cause. Look at it this way, try to see it as a redistribution of wealth. It's good for a society to have its wealth redistributed from time to time. Otherwise you wind up like the Egypt of the Pharaohs—a few tycoons eating chili and caviar in their plush houseboats on the Nile, and everybody else straining their milk shoving big slabs of granite around the desert. Does that make sense to you? Is this an ideal society?"

"How am I supposed to go back there with an eight-by-ten glossy of those kids?"

He raised the pork chop thoughtfully, then bit into it. "Well, amigo, you won't have to. This was just a practice run. I'll develop and print that film and see what you came up with. Consider it basic training. Boot camp. This is boot camp."

Boot camp lasted a week. Billetdoux was a good salesman. He almost always got into a house, and when he didn't, he vowed to me that he'd come back with a vengeance. I didn't ask him what he meant because I'd begun to suspect that he was crazy. I guess I would have quit after that session with the kids, but I figured that once I was out on my own his activities and mine would be separate. He was a thief, he was crazy, but I wasn't. He would develop and print my

138

film and pay me my commissions and that would be the extent of our relationship. I wanted the job badly enough to gloss over my own objections. I liked the idea of taking pictures door to door. It was better than working in a saw mill or on a road crew or baling hay for some stingy farmer. I'd be out in nice neighborhoods every day, I'd meet interesting people, no foreman looking over my shoulder, no time clock to punch.

The last day of boot camp Billetdoux parked his car—a 1939 Chevy whose interior smelled of moss— at the edge of the most exclusive neighborhood in town, Bunker Hill Estates. "Top of the world, amigo," he said, sipping black wine from a square bottle. The neighborhood was lush and hilly, the houses sprawling and surrounded by vast, perfectly tended lawns. "The land of the Pharaohs, amigo," he said. "Makes me jumpy, going up against them. I need this little bracer." He offered the bottle to me and I took a sip. It was sweet, thick wine, like cough syrup.

We got out of the car and started walking up the steep street toward the looming estates of Bunker Hill. Billetdoux began laboring right away, wheezing, barely able to put one foot in front of the other. I was carrying all the equipment, but he acted as if he had the full load. "I don't feel so hot, amigo," he said, stopping next to a tall bushy hedge. His face had gone white, his mouth a torn pocket: The Mask of Tragedy. There was a short picket fence on the street side of the hedge. Immediately behind the fence was a narrow flower bed, then the hedge. Billetdoux stepped over the fence and into the flowers. "I'm sick," he said. He unbuckled his belt. He took off his jacket and handed it to me. He dropped his pants and squatted into the hedge until only his pale, stricken face was showing. A dark eruption of bowel noise broke the tranquil air. Billetdoux sighed. "Lord," he said. "What a relief. Must have been that goddamned chokecherry wine." He smiled weakly. I stood there, holding his jacket, the full weight of the incredible situation beginning to impress itself on me. A small dog, alerted by the commotion, came snapping up to Billetdoux. The dog was perfectly groomed. It looked like a blond wig that had come to life. Billetdoux put a hand out to it, to appease it or to ward it off, and the dog bit his finger. Billetdoux fell backwards into the hedge, disappearing. The dog went after him, lusting for blood after his initial success with this hedge-fouling trespasser. Then they both emerged, Billetdoux roaring to his feet, the dog in frenzied attack. "Son of a bitch," Billetdoux said, picking the dog up roughly by its collar, a satiny bejeweled affair. "I hate small dogs like this, don't you amigo? Probably eats anchovies and cake."

140

I looked up and down the street, expecting a crowd of curious Bunker Hill residents attracted by the ruckus, but the street remained empty and serene. I was in awe before that unperturbed serenity. It was the serenity of people who knew who they were, enjoyed it, and who believed in their basic indispensibility to the great scheme of things. Pharaohs. Serene Pharaohs untouched by the small and large calamities that nipped at the heels of people like Billetdoux and me.

I turned back to Billetdoux. He was squatting back into the hedge, the dog firmly in his hand. "I really hate these lap dogs," he said, "but sometimes they come in handy."

"What are you *doing?*" I said. But I could see very well what he was doing. He was using the small dog for toilet paper.

"It's all they're good for, dogs like these," he said, a sinister joy playing on his lips. "Bite my jewels, you little pissant, and I'll feed you to the flowers."

141

The dog whined pitifully. Billetdoux tossed it aside and stood up. The dog burrowed into the thick hedge, making a shrill whistling noise. "I feel much better, thanks," Billetdoux said to no one's inquiry as he buckled up. I handed him his jacket and he slipped it on, squaring his shoulders in the manner of someone who has just finished important business and is ready for the next challenge. He stepped over the picket fence. "Well, don't just stand there, amigo. Time, like the man said, is money."

We continued up the street, stopping, finally, at the crest of the hill. Billetdoux leaned on a mail drop. "Look," he said, "you can see the whole town from up here. Lovely, no? See the smoke from the mills? See the pall it makes across the town's humble neighborhoods? Wouldn't it be nice to live up here where the air is pure, where all you can smell is flowers and money? What do you think, amigo? Think I should buy a house up here, with the Pharaohs?"

"Sure," I said, thinking of the ten bucks I loaned him that first day, the twenty I'd loaned him since, thinking of his wife and child, his wrecked yard, his mildewed Chevy.

He laughed bitterly. "No way, amigo. I couldn't take it. Too stuffy, if you know what I mean. A man couldn't be himself up here. I'd wind up playing their game . . . Who's Got It Best."

We walked along a narrow, tree-lined street called Pinnacle Drive. Billetdoux pointed at the street sign. "Here we are—the top of the world. The Pinnacle. Everything is downhill from here. That's the definition of *pinnacle*, isn't it? Isn't that what they're trying to tell us? You're damn straight it is."

It might have been true. The houses were two and three stories and wide as aircraft hangars. Giant blue-green lawns were fitted with precise landscaping. Three to four cars gleamed in every garage.

We stopped at the biggest house on Pinnacle Drive, a slate gray, four-story saltbox affair with a seven-foot wrought iron fence surrounding it.

"What do you see, amigo," Billetdoux said, his voice cagey.

"A nice house."

"A nice house he says. Look again, amigo. It's a monument, dedicated to arrogance, greed, and the status quo."

I looked again. I saw a nice house with a long sloping

lawn studded with beautiful shrubs, a piece of metal sculpture—a seal or possibly a bear—curled at the base of a fine elm.

"You're stone blind," Billetdoux said when I told him this. "You'll never be a real photographer. You've got scales on your eyes. Stick to mothers and babies—don't take up real picture-taking. Promise me that, will you?"

Billetdoux stepped up onto the stone retaining wall that held the iron fence. He grabbed the bars and began to yell. "Hey! You in there! We're on to you! We smell your goddamned embalming fluid, you fat-assed Egyptian mummies!" He began to laugh, enormously entertained by his performance.

Twin Dobermans came galloping up to the fence. The drapes of the front room moved. The Dobermans leaped at the fence, going for Billetdoux's hands. "I bet they've got us covered with tommy guns," he said, stepping off the retaining wall. "Look at those front doors, amigo. Eight-feet tall and wide enough to run a double column of storm troopers through them. Now tell me, do you honestly feel there is warm human activity blundering around behind those dead-bolted doors? No you don't. Tight-assed, nasty, withered old Pharaoh and his Pharaohette live in there, stinking the place up with embalming fluid. Christ, amigo, it turns my stomach." He sat down suddenly on the retaining wall and covered his face with his hands. His shoulders heaved, as if racked with sobs, but he made no sound. "Lona is sick," he said, half-whispering. "That's why I steal

143

things. You called it right kid, I'm a thief." He looked at me, his face fighting a severe emotion that threatened to dissolve it. "These people get a head cold and they fly to the Mayo clinic. I can't even buy medicine for Lona." He took out his handkerchief and mopped his face with it. "Give me the Argus, amigo. I'll show you how to take a picture."

I opened the equipment case and handed him the camera. He began snapping pictures of the house. The drapes of the front room moved gently as if the house was suddenly filled with soft breezes.

144

"I'm looking at those doors," he said, sighting through the camera. "I'm looking at the shadow that falls across them on a severe diagonal due to the over-hang above the steps. The effect, amigo, is grim. Now I'm sliding over to the left to include a piece of that window. This is interesting. This is the geometry of fear—a specialty of the Egyptians." He snapped a few more pictures, then handed me the camera. "Every-thing makes a statement, whether it wants to or not," he said. "It's up to you, as a photographer, to see and record it—in that order. *Seeing,* amigo, that will come with maturity."

Billetdoux was full of himself. His eyes were shining with the power and accuracy of his perceptions. He looked stronger and more self-confident and even healthier than ever. He looked brave and intelligent and generous and sane. I raised the Argus and took a picture of him.

The front doors of the house opened. A tall, silver-haired man in a jumpsuit came down the steps shading his eyes to see us better. Seeing their master approach, the Dobermans renewed their attack. They leaped at the fence, turned full circles in midair, came down stiff-legged and gargling with rage.

"Down Betsy, down Arnold," said the silver-haired man when he reached us. "Is there something I can do for you gentlemen?" he asked, a charming smile on his handsome face. He was elegant and calm and genuinely undisturbed by us.

Billetdoux shoved his hand through the bars of the fence, offering it to the old man. "We're doing some freelancing for the *Clarion,*" he said. I waved the camera for proof.

145

"Ah, journalists," said the man, dignifying us.

"Right," Billetdoux said, grinning horribly.

"Well, why don't you come inside and take some pictures of our antiques? Nedda, my wife, is a collector."

Billetdoux looked at me, his face so deadpan that I almost giggled. We followed the old man along the fence to the main gate. He sent the dogs away and then let us in.

The man's wife, Nedda, showed us through the house. It was tastefully furnished with antiques. The dry, musty smell of old money was everywhere. It rose up in the dust from the oriental carpets. It fell from the handsomely papered walls. It lived in the stately light that slanted into the rooms from the tall windows. It was a friendly, bittersweet smell, like stale chocolate, or maybe like the breath of a Pharaoh.

After the tour, we were given ham sandwiches and

coffee, along with coleslaw. Nedda brought a tray of wonderfully frosted cookies and refilled our coffee cups. Then we toured the house again, the fourth floor where Nedda kept her most prized antiques. Billet-doux, still playing the journalist, snapped a dozen flash pictures. He was working with a kind of controlled panic, on the verge of breaking an avaricious sweat. His jacket pocket clinked with dead flash bulbs.

Then we went downstairs, exchanged a few more pleasantries, and left. "Guess you were wrong about them," I said.

He brushed the air between us with his hand. "Petty bourgeois front, amigo. Don't kid yourself."

"What's wrong with Lona?" I asked, surprising myself.

He shrugged. "The twentieth century," he said. "It depresses her. She's very sensitive."

"Oh," I said.

"You think being depressed is a picnic?" he said, annoyed at my tone. "It's an illness, amigo, serious as cancer."

"Really," I said.

He looked at me strangely, then slapped his stomach hard. He made a loud barking sound.

"What's wrong?" I asked.

"I can't eat coleslaw. The bastards put out coleslaw." We were halfway to the front gate. "I can't make it, amigo. Let's head back." He turned quickly and headed back toward the front doors. The Dobermans didn't come after us, though I expected them to come sailing

146

around the house at any second. Billetdoux, doubled over and barking, ran up the steps of the front porch. He rang the bell until the door opened.

"The journalists," said the pleasant old man.

"Please," Billetdoux grunted. "Can I use your facilities?"

"Most certainly," said the old man. "Do come in."

The old man led Billetdoux away. I waited in the foyer. Nedda saw me. "Oh, you're back," she said.

"Yes, ma'am," I said. "My boss had to use your bathroom. He can't eat coleslaw."

She touched her cheek with her fingers. "Oh dear," she said. "I'm so sorry. I hope he isn't too distressed. Would you like some candy while you're waiting?"

"Yes, ma'am," I said. So these are the Pharaohs, I thought.

She went out and came back with a box of chocolates. I studied the brown shapes then selected one I hoped was filled with cream instead of a hard nut.

"Oh take *more*," she said, holding the box closer to me. "Fill your pocket. I'm not allowed them anyway. Neither is Burton."

Billetdoux came in, smelling of expensive cologne. "Let's hit the road, amigo," he said. "We've bothered these fine people long enough."

"No bother at all," said Nedda. "We don't get much company these days. I'm glad you came. Do drop in again."

Out on the street Billetdoux said, "Christ, what a pair of phonies. I thought we'd never get out of there."

147

"Better check your wallet," I said.

He looked at me sharply but didn't say anything. I popped a chocolate into my mouth. Mint cream. I didn't offer him one. He reached into his pocket and took out a small sculpture of a Chinese monk lifting a wineskin to his grinning lips.

"Look at this piece of junk," he said. "I thought it was some kind of special jade, white jade maybe, but it's only soapstone. Chances are all those antiques are phonies, too." He tossed the guzzling monk into a shrub as we walked downhill toward his car.

148

After my first one-hundred-dollar week, Billetdoux invited me over to celebrate my success. "You're on your way, amigo," he said, uncapping a quart of cheap vodka. He made us a pair of iceless screwdrivers and we clinked glasses before drinking. "Here's to the hotshot," he said. "Here's to the man with the charm."

We drank half a dozen screwdrivers before we ran out of frozen orange juice. Then we switched to vodka on the rocks, minus the rocks. His mood changed as we got drunk.

"Here's to the hotdog capitalist," he said, turning ugly. "Here's to J. P. Morgan Junior."

He spread the photographs of Nedda's antiques out on the table before us. "There could be some money in these items, amigo. Enough to finance my retirement. Enough to escape the twentieth century. Unless they're fakes." He looked at me then, his eyes hard and rock steady. "How about it, amigo?"

"How about what?" I said, thick-tongued.

"How about we take it. How about we pay a mid-night visit to Pinnacle Drive and get us a truckload of antiques?"

My mouth was already dry from the vodka, but it went drier. "No way," I said. "I'm a photographer, not a felon."

"Photographer my suffering ass!" he said. "You just don't have the belly for it, amigo. Look at yourself. You're about to muddy your drawers." He laughed happily, poured more vodka. My stomach rumbled on cue, and he laughed again.

149

Dinner was a blistered pizza that was both soggy and scorched. Shyanne made it from a kit. She cut it into eight narrow slices. Billetdoux and I ate at the kitchen table. Shyanne carried a tray into Lona's bedroom, then went into the living room with her two slices of pizza to watch TV.

"I should have gotten some T-bones," Billetdoux said.

"No, this is fine," I said.

"Don't bullshit a bullshitter, amigo," he said.

To change the subject, I told him about some of my weirder customers. I told him about the old weightlift-ing champ who posed for me in a jockstrap, holding a flowerpot in each hand to make his biceps bulge. I told him about the couple who took turns sitting on each other's lap, touching tongues. Then there was the crackpot who wore a jungle hat and spoke German at a full shout to a photograph of his dead wife.

Billetdoux wasn't amused. "You think the human condition is a form of entertainment for us less unfortunate citizens, amigo?" he said. "Remember, 'There but for the grace of God go I.'"

I thought about this for a few seconds. "Sometimes it is," I said, refusing to buckle under to his hypocritical self-righteousness. "Sometimes it's entertaining as hell."

He glowered at me, then brightened. "Hey, come out to the garage with me. I want to show you something."

150   I stood up, felt the floor tilt and rotate, sat back down. When the room stabilized itself, I got up again.

Outside, the air was crisp. A cold wind seemed to be falling straight down out of the sky. Billetdoux opened the garage door and switched on the lights. "Ta da!" he sang.

A long, pearl gray car gleamed in the overhead light. "Wow," I said, honestly moved. "What is it?"

"That is a *car*, amigo," he said. "It's a 1941 LaSalle. I got it for a song from an old lady who didn't know what she had. It's been in storage—only eleven thousand miles on it."

We got in. The interior was soft, dark gray plush. Even the door, when it latched, sounded like money slapping money. Billetdoux started it and backed out onto his lawn.

"It's a little dusty," he said, getting out of the car. "I'm going to hose it off. Dust will murder a finish like this."

I went back into the house. I found the vodka and

poured some into my glass. Noise, like a mob of crows in flight, passed through the kitchen. I looked out the kitchen window. Billetdoux was leaning against the front fender of the LaSalle. He saw me and winked. He began to undulate, as if performing sex with the car. "I think I'm in love," he shouted.

What sounded like a mob of raucous crows was actually Lona. She was singing in a language that might have been Egyptian. She could have been strumming her guitar with a trowel for all the music that was coming out of it. Then a tremendous crash shook the house. Glass tinkled.

Billetdoux came in. "Are they at it again?" he asked me. Glass shattered. Wood splintered. "Oh oh," he said.

Oh oh seemed like a totally failed response to the din. Billetdoux sighed weakly. "I smell trouble," he said.

We poured ourselves some vodka. The uproar changed in character. Two voices were now harmonizing in throat-tearing screams. Now and then something made the walls shake.

"Maybe we'd better have us a look," he said, sipping.

I sipped too. Outside the kitchen window, the perfect LaSalle gleamed like a classy rebuttal to human life.

We went to the back of the house. Lona's bedroom door was open. For a second or two I didn't understand what I was looking at. What I saw was Lona and Shyanne kneeling face to face on the bed, combing each other's hair. A dresser was lying on its side and a mirror was on the floor cracked diagonally in half. I

151

saw, then, that neither one of them had combs in their hands. Just great knots of hair. Lona was growling through her clenched teeth and Shyanne was *hissing.* Shyanne's mouth was very wide and the teeth were exposed. She looked like a cheetah. Then they fell over and rolled to the floor. They rolled toward us and we stepped back, holding our drinks high. The air before us was filled with flailing legs and whipping hair. "Knock it off, okay?" Billetdoux suggested meekly. He watched them a while longer, then set his drink on the floor. "Give me a hand, will you, amigo?" he said.

He grabbed Shyanne under the armpits and lifted her off Lona. She continued to kick out at Lona as Billetdoux pulled her into the hall. I reached for a waving leg, then thought better of it. Lona got heavily to her feet. Her gray hair had shapes wrung into it. Horns, knobs, antennaes. Lumps that suggested awful growths. She picked up a lamp and flung it at Shyanne who was no longer in the room. It exploded against the wall, next to my head. "God damn you to hell," she said to me, but meaning, I think, Shyanne.

"Fat witch! Pus hole! Slop ass!" Shyanne yelled from somewhere else in the house.

After things quieted down, Billetdoux fixed us a new round of drinks. Vodka and warm apricot nectar. "That was intensely embarrassing, amigo," he said. "They go ape shit about once a month or so. Don't ask me why."

I made some kind of suave gesture indicating the futility of things in general, but it didn't come off well since I was barely eighteen and hadn't yet earned the right to such bleak notions. I pulled in my gesturing hand so that it could cover my mouth while I faked a coughing fit.

But Billetdoux wasn't paying any attention to me. "The television, the guitar," he said. "This house is too small for us. They tend to get on each other's nerves. Sometimes it comes to this."

I was drunk enough to say, "How come you let your daughter treat her mother that way?"

Billetdoux looked at me. "My daughter?" he said. "What are you saying, amigo?"

"Your daughter, Shyanne, she . . ."

"My *daughter?* You think I'm beyond insult, amigo? You think we've reached a point in time where anything at all can be said to Price Billetdoux?" For the first time he pronounced his name in accurate French.

"She's *not* your daughter?" I said, thoroughly numb to the hard-edged peculiarities of Billetdoux's life, but somewhat surprised anyway.

"*Damn,*" he said, glumly.

"Then Lona . . ."

"Lona? Lona? Jesus, amigo, what godawful thing are you going to say now?"

"I thought Lona was your wife."

"Lona," he said, measuring his words, "is my Mom." His voice was dark with a dangerous reverence that adjusted my frame of mind for the rest of the evening.

Shyanne came into the kitchen. She opened the fridge and took out a bottle of Upper Ten. She made a

153

face at Billetdoux then at me. "Oh baby baby," Billet-doux said, his voice wounded with love.

"I think you should tell her to move out," Shyanne said.

"Oh, baby. No. You know I can't do that. It would kill her."

"How do you think *I* feel?" she said. "Maybe you want *me* to move out. Is that what you want?" Her small red lips puckered into a hard, toy doll pout. "I'll *go*. I'll just *go*."

"Don't say that, baby," Billetdoux said, miserably.

Shyanne still looked twelve years old to me. But the hard unwavering stare she had leveled at me was not something a child was capable of. I moved her age up to sixteen or seventeen. But something older by five thousand years hung stupidly in her face.

"Say the word, I'll go. I'll pack," she said.

I went out into the front room as Billetdoux began to weep on the small breast of his teenage wife.

I switched the TV to "The Perry Como Show." I watched it all. Then I switched to "Wagon Train." I had ignored the sounds coming from the kitchen—the soft, sing-song assurances, the cooing words that dissolved into groaning embraces, the serious oath-making, the baby talk threats, and, finally, the mindless chit-chat.

Billetdoux came in and sat down on the couch next to me. He was eating a peanut butter sandwich and drinking beer. "What can I say, amigo?" he said. "Are you going to think of me now as an old cradle robber?

Hell, I'm only thirty-eight. Shyanne's almost sixteen. You think that's too young?"

I shrugged. "What's a dozen years more or less," I said, my arithmetic deliberately sentimental.

He straightened up, set his sandwich and beer down on the coffee table. "My situation is not easy, amigo. I'm so crazy about Shyanne. I can't live without her. You understand? No, you don't. Maybe someday you will, if you get lucky. At the same time, I've got to think about Lona. I can't set her adrift after all she's done for me, can I?"

"No," I said, remembering to be careful.

Billetdoux was chewing his lower lip and absent-mindedly cracking his knuckles. "Mom thinks the world of me," he said. "Did I tell you that? She calls me her Honey Boy."

I went back to the kitchen to get myself an Upper Ten. My stomach felt like I'd swallowed a cat. Shyanne was still at the table. She was looking at her hands, studying first the tops, then the bottoms.

"They're red," she said, without looking up. "I hate these hands. Look at them. They're not very elegant, are they?"

I got my Upper Ten, opened it.

"I'm sick of my hands," she said. "I'd just as soon cut them off."

She tried to show me her hands, but I walked past them and back to the living room. Billetdoux was pacing in front of the TV. "I'm going to Carnuba the

155

LaSalle," he said. "It's been on my mind." He stalked out, like a man with pressing business.

I sipped my pop. Some kind of detective show was on now. After a while, Shyanne came in and sat next to me. Lona was strumming her guitar again and singing in Egyptian. "Are you going to take me fishing or not?" Shyanne said, her lips brushing my ear. Her tone of voice made me feel as though I'd broken every promise I'd ever made.

"Did I say I would?" I said.

"No one's taken me fishing since we came to this dumb town."

I noticed she was sitting on her hands.

"I know what you're thinking," she said, turning her face sidelong to mine. "I know *exactly* what you're thinking."

I got up and went outside. Billetdoux was out on the lawn rubbing wax into the gleaming LaSalle. He was holding a flashlight in one hand and buffing with the other. "Amigo," he said. "Loan me twenty before you go, okay? I'm in a bit of a jam."

I gave him twenty without comment and walked away. I felt, then, that I'd seen enough of the Billetdoux family and that I wouldn't be back, ever.

But half an hour later I was in his kitchen again for no reason other than a vaguely erotic curiosity. I made myself another vodka and nectar and took it out to the back yard. It was a clear, moonless night. *The moon,* I thought, *is in Egypt.*

I sat on the dead grass and drank until I got sick. The

sickness was sudden and total and my stomach emptied itself colossally into the lawn. When I was able to sit up again, I saw Lona. She was standing before the open bedroom window, naked, her strangely tranquil face upturned to the sky. Her eyes were closed and she was holding her arms out in front of her, palms up, in a gesture that reminded me of ancient priestesses. Her big silver breasts gleamed in the chilly starlight.

"Honey Boy," she said, her eyes still closed, her face still raised to the delicate radiations of the night. "Honey Boy, come here."

157

I got up heavily. I thoroughly believed in that moment that I had once again decided to leave. But I found myself walking trancelike to *Lona.* Like an inductee to a great and lofty sect, having passed my preliminary ordeal, I moved, awestruck, as if toward the sphinx.

Previous Winners of the Drue Heinz Literature Prize

The Death of Descartes, by David Bosworth, 1981
Dancing for Men, by Robley Wilson, Jr., 1982
Private Parties, by Jonathan Penner, 1983
The Luckiest Man in the World, by Randall Silvis, 1984
The Man Who Loved Levittown, by W. D. Wetherell, 1985